On Level Ground

On Level Ground

A DAVIS MORGAN MYSTERY

Danny & Wanda Pelfrey

CrossLink Publishing

CrossLink Publishing
558 E. Castle Pines Pkwy, Ste B4117
Castle Rock, CO 80108
www.crosslinkpublishing.com

Ordering Information:
Quantity sales. Special discounts are available on quantity purchases by corporations, associations, and others. For details, contact the "Special Sales Department" at the address above.

On Level Ground/ Pelfrey —1st ed.

Printed in the United States of America. All rights reserved under International Copyright Law.

ISBN 978-1-63357-114-3

Library of Congress Control Number: 2017947065

All scripture quotations are taken from THE HOLY BIBLE, NEW INTERNATIONAL VERSION®, NIV® Copyright © 1973, 1978, 1984, 2011 by Biblica, Inc.™ Used by permission. All rights reserved worldwide.

This book is a work of fiction. Names, characters, businesses, organizations, places, events and incidents either are the product of the author's imagination or are used fictitiously. Any resemblance to actual persons, living or dead, events, or locales is entirely coincidental.

CHAPTER 1

Davis was at the wheel with Deidre in the passenger seat. The red Jeep Wrangler moved at a leisurely pace as it traveled east out of Adairsville toward the small community of Pine Log. "Did you call Mrs. Taylor to get permission to visit with her?" Deidre questioned.

"No, I didn't. At her age, Bessie doesn't get out much anymore, so we should catch her at home, and she's always delighted to have visitors. No need to make an appointment." The newly-married couple had returned five days earlier from cold Cape Cod where they spent their week-long honeymoon, and Davis was still trying to catch up on his work. Wearing several hats made that chore difficult. Davis, for more than twenty years a successful pastor, was now the interim pastor for his home church in Adairsville where he also operated the Corra Harris Bookshop, and served as the volunteer chaplain for the police department. Because he had some experience as a writer, and deep roots in his hometown, the city fathers asked him to write a history of their town. That assignment needed to be finished soon, and he wasn't sure when he could get back to it.

Davis was determined that, where it was possible, he would give priority to his work with the church. It was that commitment that had them traveling in the direction of Pine Log toward the end of a busy day.

"Do you know why Mrs. Taylor wants to see you?" Deidre asked.

"No, I was told only that she wasn't well and would like to have the preacher come for a visit. I suspect she needs a little encouragement. Amy and I visited with her a couple of days before the wedding when I picked up some old books she gave me for the shop."

"Was there anything special in that batch of books?"

"No, I don't think so, though I haven't had time to sit down to carefully examine them yet. They're in my storage closet at the shop. I'll get to them in a couple of days." Davis was delighted that his beautiful dark-haired wife could accompany him on this pastoral call. Five days a week, she was a popular history teacher at Adairsville High School. Fortunately, she had been able to arrange a week off for the honeymoon trip, but that extended time away from her job eliminated the possibility of available days in the immediate future.

"I really don't know Mrs. Taylor. Because of her poor heath, she has been able to be in church very little in the year and a half that I have been there. I went with a group last Christmas to carol and deliver her a fruit basket. She seems to be a happy lady with a delightful personality, but I've never really talked with her," Deidre remarked.

"You'll enjoy getting to know her. She's had an interesting life."

"Why do you say that? What is it about her life that makes it interesting?" Deidre asked her husband. Davis, a native of Adairsville, probably knew more about its people than just about anyone other than Miss Helen Townsend. Like Miss Helen, Davis could go on for hours about the people he had loved and found fascinating for so long. Mrs. Taylor was one of those people.

"How much do you know about Corra Harris, other than that I named my bookshop after her?" Davis asked as he slowed down to take a rather severe curve in the road.

"I know she was an early twentieth-century author who wrote around twenty books, most of them novels typical of the times. Her most successful novel was *The Circuit Rider's Wife*, which was made into a movie in the fifties and starred Susan Hayward.

It was retitled *I'd Climb the Highest Mountain*. That's about it. I have to admit that I don't know a great deal more about her." Deidre, who grew up in the Southern end of the state where people had pretty much forgotten the early twentieth century author, confessed.

"There's much more, such as her role as the first American female foreign war correspondent during WWI. She was sort of the queen of the lady's magazines, and a well-known author in her day, but I guess none of that is too important to what I'm about to tell you about Bessie Taylor. We'll turn left another mile or two down the highway onto Pleasant Road. Corra Harris's house, an expanded Indian cabin, will be on a hill to the right, a mile or two along that road. Bessie grew up in a house on the left side of that same road, probably less than two miles from the Harris place. Bessie's childhood home burned to the ground a long time ago, but in more recent years she has lived in a small cottage just a mile or so past where she spent her early life." At that point, a deer ran across the road in front of them which caused Davis to brake suddenly.

Deidre watched the deer cross, "So, in her childhood, she was a neighbor of the famous author," she suggested.

"Well, there's more to it than that. Mrs. Harris moved to this area after her preacher husband died while a visitor in the community. She had only one child, a daughter named Faith, who was already an adult and lived in Nashville when Corra came to live here. Faith, always in poor health it seems, died very young, which left Corra a terribly lonely lady. One day in the early nineteen-thirties, Mrs. Harris spotted the energetic little girl, probably not yet school age as she ran and played alone in a field near her home. Mrs. Harris approached the little girl who seemed to have a gift for conversation, and found a new friend. Bessie spent many hours over a three or four-year time-period with the previously lonely lady. They were constant companions after that day. I've heard stories of Corra on trips to the Adairsville drug store in her shiny black Ford automobile to pick up her prescriptions with the lively elf of a girl at her side. The friendship, between the two continued until the author died in 1935." Davis turned left onto Pleasant Road before he accelerated again.

"So, Bessie had the opportunity to not only be a neighbor to a famous author, but also became the granddaughter she never had." Deidre surmised.

"That sums it up well, but the beauty of it is that Bessie not only had the opportunity to rub shoulders with Corra Harris, but because of that relationship was able to meet some of the most important people of her time. There are accounts of Corra Harris's Saturday afternoon teas that included guests from the Atlanta Journal. For several years, late in life, Corra wrote a tri-weekly Atlanta Journal column called *Candlelit*. She often entertained people like Margaret Mitchell who wrote for the Journal's Sunday Magazine in her pre-*Gone with the Wind* days, Martha Berry, the founder of Berry College, and even her friend Henry Ford, who occasionally showed up for these retreats. There were others, and Bessie met them all when she assisted Mrs. Harris with those events. The little country girl became a friend to some of the greatest achievers of that day."

Davis pointed to the right and slowed down a bit. "You can't see it from here for the trees, but the Harris house is just atop that hill," Davis told his young wife. "It's gone through several owners since nineteen-thirty-five. In more recent years it became the pet project of a local businessman who restored the house, grounds, library and chapel back to their former glory. Today it's in the hands of a state university."

Two or three minutes later they made a left turn to enter the long gravel drive that led to Bessie's house. Up ahead, perhaps less than a hundred yards, Davis saw a figure run across the narrow drive to enter the woods on the other side and then disappear. It was the way the person was dressed that caught Davis's attention.

"Did you see that?" He bellowed. "That person who ran across the road wore a black hoodie. Do you think that could be the Adairsville Creeper?"

"I just caught a glimpse of him, and it did appear he had on a black hoodie, but I guess people other than the Creeper own black sweatshirts with hoods. It's a rather cool day," Deidre added.

"You may be right, but I would think most local people who have them would keep them stored away in light of the news reports of the mysterious Creeper in the black hood. A guy could get shot wearing a black hoodie around here." Davis wondered if he should call Charley Nelson, his young policeman friend to report what he had seen, but reluctantly decided to let it go.

Before he got out of their vehicle in front of Bessie's neat little bungalow, Davis told Deidre, "As I remember, Bessie has a watch dog that makes a lot of noise, but he won't hurt us."

When she heard that news, Deidre slowed down to walk a step or two behind Davis. When they climbed the three steps to walk onto the small porch with an old fashion porch swing on one end and a lot of potted flowers scattered about, they spotted the dog asleep near the front door. "Wake up boy, you've got visitors." Davis, who didn't want to surprise the large longhaired dog, raised his voice, but the brownish canine continued to lay in the same spot. Davis was unsure as to whether he should reach down and pet the dog. He liked having five fingers on each hand and didn't want to lose any of them, so he again called to the dog, "Wake up pooch, you've got guests." Still the dog continued to lie still, and then Davis noticed there was no slight in and out movement of the dog's side or stomach as one would expect to see when a large dog is asleep. The pet didn't seem to be breathing.

Davis threw caution to the wind to reach down and pet the head of Bessie's watchdog. There was no response even when Davis moved his hand down the back of the animal. "This dog is dead! We'd better check on Bessie," Davis stammered. He quickly stepped over the body of the dead dog to vigorously pound on the front door, and call out with a loud voice, "Bessie, are you home?" He called a second time, and waited for a response. Then once again he yelled, "Bessie, are you all right?"

After he gave adequate time even for a ninety-year-old to respond, and still there was no reply, Davis told Deidre, "You wait here, I'll go try the back door." Davis was almost running when he went past Deidre, and down the steps before he disappeared around the corner. He found the backdoor, and knocked loudly on the locked door while he called out to his longtime friend, "Bessie, it's Davis, can you let me in?" Still no response!

Davis hurried back to the front porch where Deidre waited. "No luck?" she questioned.

"No response," Davis told her with concern in his voice. After he tried to turn the doorknob without success, Davis stated, "I'll break one of the windowpanes in this door to see if I can reach the lock on the inside." Davis looked around for an object he could use to break the window. He picked up one of the small potted plants on the porch and used the bottom of it to break one of the lower panes, He reached through the broken glass with his right hand to release the lock and open the door.

With Deidre behind him, Davis hurried into the house. He briefly stopped in the front room to observe that it was a mess with its contents scattered all over the floor. He knew that was not typical of Bessie's house. She was a meticulous housekeeper even in her old age. Davis looked to the right and the left and then made his way through the house while Deidre remained silent in the front room. He went into a small hallway where he saw that the stairway to the attic had been pulled down and left hanging, which made it difficult to get to the bedroom. Davis's glance into the first bedroom revealed it to be as much of a mess as the living room, but no Bessie. Then he quickly made his way to the second bedroom which was in as much disarray as the other rooms. His mouth dropped open and for a moment he was frozen in silence when he looked at the space between the bed and the wall. There he spotted Bessie on her stomach with blood all over her head. "Deidre," he screamed. "Call 911, I've found Bessie. We need an ambulance and the police."

CHAPTER 2

By the time Deidre got into the bedroom, Davis had turned Bessie onto her back. He snatched a pillow from the bed and put it beneath her bloody head. "Is she dead?" Deidre reluctantly asked. She stood several feet away with a frightened look on her face.

"No, she's still breathing, but I hope the EMTs get here quickly. She's badly injured, and at her age, a blow to the head like this could, no doubt, be fatal."

The Bartow County EMTs did arrive quickly, since they had only about five miles to travel. Davis met them on the front porch to point the pair of medical professionals in the right direction. The one who led the way, a slender young lady who reminded Davis of his daughter Amy, stepped over the dead dog and asked, "What happened to this animal?"

"I don't know, we found him this way when we got here about fifteen minutes ago," Davis told her.

When they entered the bedroom, they found Deidre on her knees on the floor beside Bessie. "It's okay, the EMTs are here. They'll take care of you," she said to the unconscious lady on the floor before she got up to allow the professionals space to do their work.

One of the EMTs took vitals while the other examined the wound on Mrs. Taylor's head. "Did she fall?" the male member of the medical team asked.

"We don't know what happened. When we got here, we found the dog dead on the porch and Bessie here on the floor with a bloody head."

"Are you family?" one of the EMTs asked as he glanced toward Davis and Deidre.

"No, I'm her preacher. Bessie hasn't been well. We're here for a pastoral visit."

"Looks like it was a good idea for you to make that visit," the attendant said before he again turned his attention to Mrs. Taylor.

Davis and Deidre moved to the front room to get out of the way. After a couple of minutes, they heard a car arrive and Davis moved to the porch to meet the two Bartow County Sheriff's Deputies. Over the next ten to fifteen minutes he tried his best to answer the questions the officers threw at him. Davis remembered the person he spotted with the black hood, and told the officers about him.

"A black hood you say?" one of the officers questioned as he looked at the other. "Did you say he wore a black hood?"

"That's what I said. It was either a black or navy-blue hoodie-type sweatshirt with the hood pulled over his head. My wife also caught a glimpse of him."

"Can you tell us more about him? Perhaps about his size. How would you describe his size?"

"It all happened so quickly that I really didn't have time to think about it, and he was quite a distance away from us. I think maybe he was of average height, maybe around six feet, give or take an inch, and not slender, not hugely overweight, but not skinny either. He looked our way for a moment before he went into the woods, but he was so far away, I could see none of his facial features."

"We need to get in touch with Mrs. Taylor's family, do you know if she has immediate family in the area?" one of the officers inquired.

"I know she has both a son and a daughter and several grandchildren, but I couldn't tell you where they live or even their names. I wish I could be of more help." Then Davis remembered a fact he had momentarily forgotten. His friend, Charley, was Bessie's great-nephew.

"But I know someone who might be able to help you with that information. Mrs. Taylor is Charley Nelson's great-aunt. Charley is an Adairsville police officer."

"I know Charley," one of the county officers replied. "He's a good man. Do you know how we can get in touch with him?"

"Yes, I do. I have Charley's number here in my cell." Davis took his phone out of his pocket and called out Charley's number for one of the officers who wrote it on a pad. The Sheriff's deputy then walked outside. Davis could see he was on his phone.

Before the officer returned to the front room, the EMTs wheeled Bessie through the front door. "We'll take her to emergency over in Rome," the young woman spoke rather urgently.

"We'll follow you there," Davis told them.

"It would be best for you not to try to keep up with us," the male EMT suggested. "We need to get her there as fast as possible."

"We'll be there as quickly as we can safely get there," Davis replied.

A few moments later the ambulance with Bessie on board started down the drive toward the main road. Davis and Deidre followed while the two Bartow County officers stayed to wrap up their investigation. The last glance Davis got through the rear-view mirror before he turned right onto the main road was of the two deputies, one with the head and the other at the other end, as they carried Bessie's dog. Davis took time to silently pray for his elderly friend. *These special friends are disappearing from our midst quickly - we need her Lord. I hope it's your will to let us keep her awhile longer before you take her home.* Davis found confidence in his prayer when he remembered Psalm 93:4, a verse he learned when he was a teenager: *"Mightier than the thunder of the great waters, mightier than the breakers of the sea – the Lord on high is mighty."*

Despite the fact the emergency vehicle's siren blasted, and its lights flashed, they soon lost sight of it. The urgent drive back through Adairsville and to the Floyd Medical Center in the near-by town took forty-five or fifty minutes. When they arrived, Bessie had already been taken to one of the treatment rooms. After he checked in with the lady in the white sweater at the desk, they were seated in the area where ten or fifteen other people also anxiously awaited news from ill or injured loved ones.

"Would you like to have coffee?" Davis asked Deidre.

"That sounds good," she told her husband. "Why don't you stay here while I go get it just in case someone comes out with news about Bessie? But you'll have to give me some money since I left my purse in the car."

Davis got up to take his billfold out of his hip pocket. He gave her a five-dollar bill. "That ought to be enough for two cups of coffee," he told her.

Deidre had just disappeared around the corner when Davis heard a familiar voice behind him. "What's going on with Aunt Bessie?" Charley Nelson questioned with that authoritative policeman voice to which Davis had grown accustomed over the past year. Even though Charley was perhaps fifteen years younger than forty-seven-year old Davis, they were best friends and Charley had served as best man in his and Deidre's recent wedding.

"I assume one of the Sheriff's deputies called you," Davis said as he smiled weakly at his young friend.

"That's right," Charley told him. "I decided I'd better come on over and get the scoop first hand."

"How much did the deputy tell you?" Davis inquired.

"He only told me that evidently Aunt Bessie had fallen and seriously injured her head, and that you and Deidre found her. He also mentioned that Ole Sam, her dog, was dead. I figured even if she isn't seriously injured, she'll be fit-to-be-tied if Ole

Sam is dead. She loved that old dog about as much as she loved her children."

"Well, I'm afraid she may be seriously injured. The last we heard she was still unconscious, and I'm not sure she fell. I saw someone in a black hoodie at her place when we arrived."

Just then, the two EMTs who had so efficiently aided Bessie came through. "How's Bessie?" Davis stood up to address the two.

"She's still unconscious, and there's the possibility of a concussion," the female EMT answered. She then looked toward Charley and a big smile appeared on her face. "Is that you Charley Nelson? I've not seen you around in a couple of years," she said in a tone that seemed to express a measure of delight.

"I'm sure it hasn't been that long," Charley responded quietly, almost shyly to the attractive brunette, and that was out of character for the ladies' man Davis had grown to know and love.

"Bessie, the lady you brought in, is my great aunt. I'm here to check on her."

"I hope she gets along well. We did all we could for her, and I know the doctor taking care of her. There are none better. I hope to see you again sometime soon, Charley." the young lady remarked with a smile that almost melted the heart of even the newlywed Davis. "I hear you're now a pilot. Maybe you could take me up sometime soon."

"Yeah," Charley stammered. "I got my license a few months ago. We'll get together soon."

"So, you know her?" Davis asked as the uniformed pair went through the door. She's an attractive lady. I can't believe you didn't hit on her like every other girl you're around."

"Yeah, Tonya is a gorgeous lady, but this isn't the time. Besides, she's not the type you hit on. I have too much respect for her than to do that. We had one of those required classes together down at Kennesaw a year or so back, and we went out to lunch together a couple of times."

Deidre returned with two cups of coffee. "I didn't know you were here, Charley," she said when she handed Davis one of the cups. "I would be happy to go back and get a cup for you, if you want it."

"No, thanks. I got off duty about an hour ago, and it was a boring day. I drank enough coffee to float a battleship. I've had more than my allotment today. So, you think Aunt Bessie was the victim of a robbery?" Charley asked, when he turned to face Davis.

"As you know, I'm not an expert in such matters, but my best guess is that she was struck by someone who was after something in her house. The house was a mess, and I saw nothing she could've hit in a fall that would have produced a wound like she has on her head. I suspect someone hit her from behind with some object. Besides that, the dog dead on the front porch certainly arouses my suspicions."

"Do you think it was that Adairsville Creeper guy in the black hoodie?"

"I don't know," Davis replied. "You know more about such matters than I, but despite all we have heard about him, it has only been about him lurking in places where he has no business. We know of no real crime he's committed. But maybe this is where it starts. A ninety-plus-year-old lady would be an easy target."

"It's hard for me to believe anyone would deliberately harm such a nice elderly lady," Deidre, who had up to now sat quietly spoke up.

"You're just a little gullible, Deidre," Charley retorted. "In my work, you soon learn there are all kinds out there. It's sad, but I constantly encounter people that wouldn't think twice about pounding a nice old lady over the head for a twenty-dollar bill. Our world is full of mean and desperate people."

I wish he were wrong, but that's not the case. Davis thought. *He's right, as much as I hate to admit it. Satan is alive and well in this world and that sometimes makes it a scary place to live.* Davis felt the need to move a little closer to his wife.

"Hello, Brother." The voice was that of Dean Nelson, Charley's older brother. "You don't care what kind of company you keep, do you?" Dean, a high school friend of Davis's took every opportunity to rag his old teammate. "Any word from Aunt Bessie?"

"Nothing yet," Charley answered. "She's still unconscious and they suspect a concussion."

"I was able to get hold of Uncle Pete, but I don't know if he will show up. He's never been very reliable, and doesn't seem to be very concerned about his mother. I haven't been able to get a number for Aunt Penny, but I'll continue to try."

"What happened, anyway? How was she injured?" the auto mechanic asked.

"I'll let your brother answer those questions. Deidre and I need to go since there's someone here to watch after things," Davis announced when he got up from his seat.

"Don't let me run you off," Dean taunted.

"No way you could ever run me off," Davis countered. "I've got to preach in the morning, and I need to get home to look over my notes."

"You guys don't need to study to present a sermon, do you?" Dean suggested. "Don't you just let the Spirit guide?"

"If I let the spirit guide without any preparation, it's liable to be the *helly spirit* that guides rather than the *Holy Spirit*," Davis replied with a smile. "I don't even talk with my wife without the proper preparation. Will one of you guys call me with a report when you learn about Bessie's condition?"

"One of us will do it," Charley assured him. "Thank you for your concern for Aunt Bessie."

CHAPTER 3

While he led the Sunday service, Davis divulged no details, but told the congregation that Bessie Taylor was in the hospital with a serious injury. He announced that one of her nephews had called before the service to say that besides a cut on her head that required more than twenty stiches, she also had a rather serious concussion. He asked the church to pray for her recovery.

After the service, Davis and Deidre met Davis's daughter, Amy, along with her husband, Jay, at the Adairsville Inn for lunch. Barbara Mason and her new roommate, Randi Metcalf also joined the group. Deidre and Amy had been roommates in half of the big Victorian-style house which Davis's mother had left to him while Davis had lived on the other side of the long hallway. After Amy's marriage to Jay, Barbara, a longtime friend of Deidre's, a teacher and a widow, took Amy's spot in the apartment. Now, with Deidre married and settled in the other side of the house, Randi, the new girls' basketball coach at the high school, was Barbara's roommate. All the ladies worked together at Adairsville High School and knew one another. Lunch today would be an opportunity for Davis and Jay to learn more about Randi.

"How long have you been a teacher and a coach, Randi?" Davis asked the blond young lady.

"This is my first year in Adairsville, but I spent three years at Bremen High School as JV coach and assistant varsity coach." She told Davis.

"I hope you find our little *Norman Rockwell town* to be as delightful as we do. It's a great place to live, but I guess I'm a little bias, since I grew up here," Davis explained.

"It's okay for a small town. It's better than Bremen, but I am a city gal who grew up in Nashville. I've missed the city since I graduated from Belmont University and moved to North Georgia. I do like the fact that we are close enough to Atlanta to get there in an hour."

"I think we need to introduce her to Charley Nelson," Barbara suggested. She went on to explain to Randi, "He's a rather handsome single young man who is one of our city policemen."

"Oh, she will meet Charley. You don't think he'll let an unmarried, lovely young woman in his own age bracket come to town without checking her out, do you?" Davis said with a grin on his face. "I'm surprised she has been here this long without getting to know Charley."

"I don't think I would be interested in any kind of relationship with a small-town cop," Randi announced before she looked at her menu.

"Any girl, small-town or city, would be lucky to have a friend like Charley," Deidre muttered. "He's special, one of a kind."

The waitress appeared with her pad in hand. "Are you ready to order?" she asked. One by one they placed their orders.

"How are you coming with the restoration out at Folsom?" Barbara asked Amy and Jay who had accepted the challenge to piece back together an ancient house a few miles from town, which they had bought recently. Currently they resided in a small house on College Street, a rental, while they worked on their dream acquisition.

"It's a lot of work," Jay, an engineer by trade told them. "It consumes a lot of time, but it'll be worth it when completed."

"Maybe when we finish, I'll get to see him occasionally. He gets home from his job in Atlanta about five thirty if he's lucky. He takes a sandwich to the house and works till about midnight.

He labors out there all-day Saturdays. Sunday is about the only time I see him," Amy explained.

"Have you found those millions in gold in the cave on the property?" Barbara asked.

Amy laughed and said, "We haven't even found the cave."

"How was Mrs. Taylor injured?" Jay inquired, as he looked toward Davis, and then took a sip from his water glass.

"We don't know for sure," Davis told his son-in-law, "but I suspect she was struck by a thief or a prowler."

"That really gets my dander up," Amy said with fire in her voice as well as her eyes. "How could anyone harm someone so nice and absolutely defenseless? Didn't Sam go after whoever harmed her?" Amy asked after a moment's consideration. "Ordinarily he won't let anyone get near her until she calls him off. When I went with you out there a few weeks back to pick up that box of books and papers, I thought Sam would get us for sure."

"It appears whoever injured Bessie might have killed Sam. We found him dead on the porch," Davis told his daughter.

"Was he shot?" Jay asked.

"I couldn't see a mark on him, but he was very dead when we got there," Davis reported.

"Maybe it was just his time. I think he was really old," Amy reasoned.

"That could be true," Davis said, "But what are the chances of Bessie being accidently injured, and Old Sam dying of natural causes at the same time? It would seem to me to be an unlikely coincidence. Someone must have been responsible."

At that moment, two waitresses, each with a tray of food, arrived to deliver their orders. After the waitresses left, those at the table joined hands to bless their food. Randi, evidently not accustom to prayer before a meal in a restaurant was, at first, obviously a little confused by the practice. "We usually pray before we eat, and we like to join hands when we do so," Davis explained and then prayed.

After the prayer, Amy reached to take a roll and asked her father, "Incidentally, did you find any Corra Harris memorabilia in that box of books and papers Bessie gave you?"

"I haven't had time to go through it yet. The box is still in my storage closet at the shop. I doubt, we'll find anything like that, since Bessie's association with Mrs. Harris was so long ago."

"Dad, don't forget that Bessie bought several boxes of papers plus odds and ends at that auction of Corra's estate about thirty or thirty-five years ago, there might be some Harris stuff in the box from that sale."

Davis noticed that the gentleman who sat with a lady at a near-by table appeared to eavesdrop on their conversation. He paid little attention to it since there was still a lot of interest in Corra Harris around Adairsville. That interest had grown recently due to the theater group at the Adairsville Opera house, located up-stairs in the 1902 Stock Exchange, where Davis's Bookshop was located. About three years back, they did their version of Har-ris's *CIRCUIT RIDER'S WIFE* for several consecutive weekends to sold-out crowds.

"Mr. Morgan, do you have any significant material related to *Gone with the Wind* in your shop? I love everything about that book, and have been a collector of memorabilia for the past cou-ple of years. I guess it is too much to hope that you might have a first edition of the book?" Randi inquired.

"Please call me Davis. *Mr. Morgan* makes me feel so old. I don't currently have a first edition. I have only had a true first, the May 1936 printing, one time. I found it in a display case in an an-tique mall in Chamblee for less than sixty dollars. It had no dust jacket, and wasn't in mint condition, but I still sold it in less than a month for almost one thousand dollars."

"Have you ever seen a signed copy?" Randi asked.

"I've held three signed copies in my hands, one of them a first, but I have never owned one. It's almost impossible to find one priced cheap enough to buy for resale," Davis explained.

"Let me know immediately if you ever get a first edition or a signed copy. I'll purchase either," the young basketball coach emphatically stated.

"If you're ready to make that kind of commitment, you must indeed be a serious collector," Davis replied.

"Very much so," Randi stated. "I'm fascinated by all that relates to the book or the movie."

"You might want to come by the shop sometime to look at what I do have. I don't have any really unusual materials, but I do have some Margaret Mitchell biographies as well as a couple of different book club editions of the novel with nice dust jackets, and a couple of 1936 editions though far removed from that May printing," Davis remarked.

They knew that people were waiting to be seated at the popular establishment, so the talkative group, while not in an unreasonable hurry, did not waste any time finishing their Sunday meal and go their separate ways.

* * *

Davis awakened from his nap in his recliner just before four-thirty. The Falcons were ahead of Tampa Bay by a touchdown before he fell asleep, but that game was over with another now on the TV screen. He wondered if Atlanta had been able to hang on to the lead. Davis could hear Deidre in the kitchen. He was thrilled. It had been awhile since he had awakened to those noises which were among the simple memories he cherished from his almost twenty-five-year marriage to Julie. Since cancer had taken her two years ago, he had missed those sounds. Now he had the gracious and lovely Deidre, and life was good again.

At times, the almost eighteen years between their ages, still worried him. There were other times when he felt a little guilty about being with another, almost as if he was betraying Julie. He knew, however, that Julie would approve. Deidre was exactly the kind of woman she would have chosen for him. His daughter not only approved, but encouraged the relationship, and most importantly, he was convinced it was the Lord who brought them together.

Deidre came into the room. When she saw that he was awake, she came over to sit on his lap. "I love you so," she said to him before she kissed him, and then laid her head on his shoulder.

"I haven't yet figured out why, but I'm glad you do," He told her, as he pulled her tighter to him. "There were several fellows, your own age with so much more to offer that you could've had. I still marvel that you choose me," Davis said and squeezed her tightly to him.

"I didn't want them. I wanted you. I know of no other guy who has more to offer than do you." Deidre assured him.

Davis wished they could remain just as they were for a time, but he knew that as Bessie's temporary pastor, he needed to get to the hospital to visit with her. He had previously loved life as a pastor, but now he remembered how annoying it could be at times to keep up with the duties that went with the job.

* * *

The young man with the four-inch scar on his right cheek answered his cell phone when he heard it play *Dixie*. "Did you have to slug that old lady? You may have killed her," the voice on the other end of the line said.

"You sent me to do a job, and that seemed the best way to get it done."

"Did you get it?"

"No, I tore that place apart, even went into the attic and found nothing like what you sent me for."

"I think I might know where it is. After dark, go to the 1902 Stock Exchange on the south end of the downtown area. Find the bookshop. There are three sections to the structure. I think you'll find the bookshop in the back of the section where the tearoom is located. There's a storage closet somewhere in the shop. You may find what we want in a box in that storage closet. Be careful, the police department is located just down the street."

"If it's there, I'll find it." The man with the scar declared before he discontinued the connection.

It's less than an hour before dark, I'd better get ready, he decided before he walked over to the bed in the motel room to pick up the black sweatshirt with the hood and pull it over his head.

CHAPTER 4

At four o'clock Davis was wide awake, and aware he wouldn't be able to go back to sleep, he got up and went to his desk to work on the town history. About an hour and a half later he heard Deidre while she prepared breakfast. He headed for the kitchen and asked his wife, "Is there anything I can do to help?"

She gave him that smile he had grown to love and said, "I've just about finished. It'll be ready in three or four minutes." After almost two years of making his own breakfast, usually a bowl of oatmeal with orange juice and a cup of coffee, it was great to have someone prepare a real meal for him, though he probably didn't need the eggs and sausage. Most of all, it was fantastic to have someone across the breakfast table, especially someone as nice to look at as Deidre. Even in the morning before she gave her hair its final touch and applied her makeup, she was beautiful.

"I love breakfast with you, but I know you enjoy time with Dean and the guys at the Little Rock once in a while. It won't bother me if you occasionally go to breakfast with your friends." Deidre told him between bites of toast.

"We've been married now for less than two weeks and you're already out to get rid of me," Davis accused with a laugh. "I might take you up on that once-in-a-while, but not very often. I can't take the abuse. Besides, you're a whole lot better to look at in the mornings than those guys," he offered.

"And along the same line, let me say to you that it worries me when you ride with Charley on patrol, but I know you're the chaplain for the department and need to give some attention to that responsibility. I guess I can deal with it if you don't do it too often."

"Don't worry, while involved with this interim ministry, I'll not have time for a lot of that sort of activity."

"I can't say that news disappoints me, but I don't want to be the reason you avoid the activities you enjoyed in the past," Deidre told him.

"More than anything else, I want to be with you." Davis assured her.

"That's what I like to hear," she said when she got up to kiss him on the forehead before she headed to the bedroom to get dressed for the day's work.

Usually, since his shop was closed on Mondays as were all the other businesses in the 1902 Stock Exchange, Davis used the day to search for those rare books that he needed to make his business a success. He had contacts south as far as Atlanta and north to Chattanooga. Occasionally he would venture over into Alabama. He knew the life of a used and rare book business was to constantly add desirable stock. However, Davis decided to stay home today to work on the history that had been assigned him. He decided to work at his desk for a couple more hours before he shaved or showered. As it almost always did, when he sat down at his desk, his cell phone rang.

"Hello, Davis Morgan speaking," he answered. He immediately recognized the voice on the line. It was Janie, the clerk at the Stock Exchange.

"Davis, I thought I needed to let you know that when I stopped by the Stock Exchange today to take care of some chores, I discovered we had a break-in last night. Whoever it was seemed to be mostly interested in your shop," the young clerk told him. "I've already called the police, but I thought you needed to know."

"Thank you, Janie, I'll be there in a few minutes." Davis showered but did not bother to shave. He dressed quickly before he jumped into the Jeep and headed for the shop. He imagined all kinds of damage in the three or four minutes it took him to get there.

An Adairsville Police cruiser was parked in front of the store when he arrived. Janie greeted him at the door with, "Sorry about this, Davis."

"Not your fault, Janie," He walked rapidly back to his shop where he found Charley along with Jed, who sometimes worked as Charley's partner.

"It doesn't look too bad," Charley surmised. "It appears they mostly confined their efforts to this closet back in the corner. Why don't you step back here and see what he took?"

Davis went into the closet, "It'll be difficult to determine what has been taken, since I don't know what was in here. This is a storage closet where I often bring boxes of books and other objects until I can get around to examining what I have and process it for the shelves." Books and papers were scattered all over the floor.

"It looks, to me, as if the thief had a specific target in mind," Charley speculated.

"They pulled some drawers out behind the counter, but I don't think they found anything there. I took all the money home when I locked up Saturday night," Janie, who had followed Davis to his shop, told them. "I haven't discovered that any other items are gone."

"It's unusual to find a thief with discriminating taste." Charley said. "Usually they will take any item of value that they can find.

Charley and Jed walked around the premises to see if they or Janie had missed anything. Jed returned to the patrol car while Charley came back to Davis's corner. "Incidentally, I saw Aunt Bessie earlier, before I went on duty, and she's making some progress. She's conscious, but still confused with an awfully bad headache," Charley reported to Davis.

"That's good news," Davis responded. "She was still out of it when I saw her late yesterday. How did you get past the ICU doors at a no-visitor time?"

"Sometimes, this uniform will get you places others can't go. But I suspect it was my charm that did the trick. That was one beautiful nurse at the desk."

"Okay, Casanova, spare me, I've heard all that before," Davis countered. "That reminds me, there's a young lady I think you should meet."

"I'll be happy to meet her if she isn't a missionary or something," Charley facetiously responded.

"A missionary is probably what you need," Davis retorted. "But this girl is no missionary. She's Barbara's new roommate. Randi Metcalf is her name, and she's the girls' basketball coach at the high school, about your age, or perhaps a couple of years younger. She is blond and very pretty. However, you'll have your work cut out for you. I don't think this one likes small-town cops."

"Sounds like a challenge," Charley said, as he perked up. "When can you arrange for me to meet her?"

"I'll work on that." Determined to take advantage of an opportunity, Davis suggested, "Maybe if you're not on duty Sunday, you could come to church and meet her there."

"That's a low blow even for you," Charley accused. "Now you are enlisting the help of blonds to try to draw me to church."

"With a guy like you, one must take any edge that comes his way," Davis offered with a smile. Davis had been thrilled to watch the positive changes in Charley's lifestyle since he had known him. He knew that Charley was more aware of his need, but he still had not given his life to the Lord. To help his friend satisfy life's greatest need was one of Davis's top priorities.

"Aunt Bessie told me she had no idea how she hurt her head. She said the last memory she had before she woke up in a hospital bed was that she bent over to pick up a pair of shoes. She said she must have fallen and hit her head, but I believe someone who had poisoned her dog hit her from behind," Charley concluded. "How could she get a cut on the back of her head when she fell forward?"

"I have no doubt you're right. When I discovered her, she was face down. There's a sadistic thief with no regard for life out there somewhere," Davis reasoned.

After Charley left the shop, Davis used the next couple of hours to put his storage closet back together. While busy at that task, he picked up a spoon off the floor with a fancy "H" engraved on the top of the handle. *This must have come out of Bessie's box. I wonder if the "H" is for Harris? Could this little spoon have belonged to Corra Harris? It probably has very little value, but if it was Corra's, it is neat to have, and it might be an indication that other objects which once belonged to her were in that box.* He put the spoon in the pocket of his jeans before he continued his work. Again, a day which Davis had intended to use to work on the town history had been rudely interrupted. He wondered if he would ever finish. Maybe he shouldn't have committed himself to that project, but he did, and now that the decision had been made, he would find a way to get it done.

* * *

Deidre's students were busy with an exam while she relaxed behind the desk at the front of the classroom. Once again, she was in the middle of a daydream. She told herself she was guilty of that way too often these days, so much to think about – to rejoice over. Life had not always been easy for her. She grew up on the edge of poverty in a broken home; she had worked hard to get a college degree. It seemed for several years, every potential romance eventually broke down for one reason or another. Had she set her sights too high? Did she expect too much of a man? She had begun to think that, until she got to know the father of her roommate, of all people. And now life was good, better than she had ever hoped. At first, she wondered, when the past was considered, how long it could last, but her attitude had rapidly changed. She would take each wonderful day and make the most of that day. She was Mrs. Davis Morgan and she enjoyed everything about the life the Lord had chosen for her. It was worth the wait, she decided.

The bell rang, and since she had a few minutes of break time, she proceeded to the teacher's lounge where she found Amy in one of the comfortable chairs. *Her stepdaughter*, she thought. Deidre almost laughed at the thought of her as a mother to someone just five years younger than herself. *She'll never be my daughter, but she'll always be my friend and my little sister.*

"Have you heard what happened at the Stock Exchange?" Amy asked when she saw Deidre.

"No, I haven't, what happened?" She asked immediately.

"One of my students told me it was broken into last night," Amy reported.

"What did they take?" Deidre asked with a concerned expression on her face. "Did they get into the bookshop?"

"I don't know. I've only heard that there was a break-in."

"I think I'll give your father a call and see if I can get more details," Deidre said as she pulled her cell phone from her pocket.

She punched Davis's number and felt the same thrill she always felt when she heard his voice after they were separated for a few hours. "Hello Honey, what's up?" he answered. Obviously, he checked the number to see who was on the line.

"I've just got word that the Stock Exchange was robbed last night. Is that true?" she asked.

"More correctly, we were robbed," he said. "Whoever did it seemed to be more interested in my storage closet than all the other merchandise there. I can't determine if they took much or even if they took anything, but they did make a big mess. Nothing to worry about, it just created a little more work for me."

"Work that you don't need right now," Deidre added.

"No big deal," Davis countered. "I don't know one single soul who died from overwork. How has your day been?"

"Evidently better than yours, I'm glad no valuables were taken. I'll see you in a couple of hours. I love you."

"And I love you," Davis added before he hung up.

CHAPTER 5

Ordinarily, Charley didn't mind suburban Atlanta traffic, but on this late Tuesday morning, Marietta traffic seemed to be worse than usual. He didn't want to be late for his lunch appointment with Jim Lipscomb. He had no clue about the nature of Mr. Lipscomb's business with him. He didn't even know who Lipscomb was, but in his phone conversation the previous day, the businessman made it sound important enough for Charley to convince the chief to rearrange his schedule to make it possible for them to meet.

It was almost eleven-forty-five when Charley pulled into the lot at Aspens Signature Steaks. *A little more upscale than Mac-Donald's,* Charley decided before he went inside for his noon appointment. When he questioned the receptionist at the front, he quickly learned that Lipscomb had already arrived, and he was escorted to the table of the dignified gentlemen of perhaps fifty or fifty-five years of age who wore an open collar and a blue blazer. "I'm Jim Lipscomb," he announced to Charley when he smiled and stood to extend his hand. "I appreciate that you honored my request on such short notice," he said, and motioned for Charley to sit down. "I'll only be in the area through today, and I wanted to talk with you while here."

"I'm glad to get together with you," Charley told him, "But you must know I'm curious about what this is all about."

"Let's go ahead and order," Lipscomb suggested when the waiter approached the table, "and then I'll explain to you why I needed to meet with you on such short notice."

After they placed their orders, Mr. Lipscomb said, "Let me tell you who I am, and how I happen to know about you. I'm a friend of Ted Mason. I've known his family for a good number of years, and for a brief time, he worked for me."

"Okay, I think I've put it together now," Charley responded. "Ted is Deidre's friend and Barbara's son, who a few months back spent a few days with us in Adairsville. You must be the "Jim" who chose to help him rather than prosecute him for theft."

"Ted is a fine young man who just got a little off track, but was certainly worth some effort," Lipscomb told Charley. "He's made some adjustments, and has done well. He met a young lady, and I wouldn't be surprised to receive a wedding announcement any day now."

Charley felt a twinge of envy when he heard that news, but did not comment. "But what does all this have to do with me?" he asked.

"The Lord has been good to me, Charley. One of the ways He has blessed me most is with my businesses. It's not because of any exceptional ability on my part, but for whatever reason, business has gone well for me for a long time. My various concerns have grown and they take me all over the country. Because it saves a great deal of time, I have my own plane. Our pilot will retire in a couple of months. I need to replace him. Ted tells me you're not only a good pilot, but also an exceptional law enforcement officer who could be valuable to me in security matters. It's important for me to recruit people I can keep for a long time; therefore, your youth appeals to me greatly. Mr. Nelson, this job will probably pay you two or three times your present salary with much better benefits than you currently receive."

"Just like that," Charley's expression and tone gave evidence that he was somewhat shocked. "Just out of the blue, you offer me this fantastic job?"

"No, Charley, I seldom make decisions just out of the blue. You've been thoroughly checked out, and I'm extremely pleased with what we have learned. You're my first choice, the only person who has been considered up to this point. Now it is up to you. You must decide if you want to accept the offer and move to Savannah, which incidentally, is a great place to live."

Those last words brought Charley back to earth. He had never had a desire to reside anywhere other than Adairsville. It had always been his home, and he had assumed it always would be.

"I don't know, Mr. Lipscomb! You make it sound awfully good, but I don't know if I could move away from my family and my friends, and I've never given any serious thought to any position other than being a policeman."

"I understand," Lipscomb responded. "You wouldn't be the man I want if you were to accept the job before you gave it some serious thought. I've prepared a file that will give you the details – compensation package, job description, etc. You take it home, study it, and give me your decision in a month," Jim said, as he pushed a folder toward him.

Charley started home rather dazed. The lunch had lasted a little more than an hour, but it turned his world upside down. How could anyone turn down a salary like that? Jim Lipscomb was an exceptional person and, no doubt, would be a great man to work for. He loved flying, and since security would be among his responsibilities, he wouldn't completely give up police work, he rationalized. This was a once in a lifetime opportunity; A man would be foolish not to seriously consider such an offer.

I'll take some time to digest all of this, he told himself. *This is one of those times when I wish I were like Davis, a praying man. He talks often about asking the Lord for direction, but I guess it would do me no good to do that. I wouldn't know where to start anyway.*

* * *

Just before he got to the Cass-White exit ramp, Charley saw, to his right that a tan Chevy pickup truck had run off the highway and crashed into a tall pine tree. Two vehicles were already stopped with a passenger from each headed toward the wrecked truck. Charley pulled off the highway and jumped out of his car. By the time they reached the wreck, he had caught the two men who had a substantial head-start on him. "Has anyone called 911?" the young policeman questioned.

"I did that before I left my car," the heavy-set gentleman answered while he breathed hard from his sprint to the accident site.

"Heavy smoke is coming from the engine. That truck could go up in flames. We'd better get him out of there," Charley urged the two men.

"Should we move an injured man?" one of them asked.

"It's better than to let him burn to death," Charley countered. He pulled his badge out of his pocket to show the two Good Samaritans.

"Let's get it done," the African American man cried out, and all three of them rapidly moved toward the truck with Charley out front. The passenger door opened when Charley pulled on it, but, unfortunately, it only opened about a foot before there was tension that brought it to a halt. It would go no farther.

"Help me, men. Let's see if we can get it open enough to get this guy out," Charley instructed. All three of them pulled, and they finally opened the door far enough to allow the passenger through the opening. The next challenge was to release him from the seat belt and air bag. When they finally got him out of the truck, they saw that he was dazed. He grunted and had blood on his face, but was still conscious. They managed to get him a hundred feet or so away from the truck and then place him on his back in the grass. It wasn't two minutes later that the truck ignited and began to burn.

"Wow," the heavy man said to Charley. "I'm glad you knew enough to get him out of the truck. He would be toast now if we hadn't pulled him out."

Charley hardly heard the compliment as he examined the injured man to see if there were any cuts that needed to be compressed. "The EMTs should be here shortly," Charley told his companions. "They'll know what to do for him."

A state patrolman arrived first with the medical rescue people right behind him. As the EMTs approached, Charley immediately recognized Tonya Willis as one of the trio.

"We've got to stop meeting this way," Tonya said as she knelt beside Charley who was in t-shirt on this cold early December day. He earlier removed his shirt which he now used to compress the wound on the head of the injured man. "I'll take over now," Tonya told him.

"Glad to see you," Charley responded when he stood to allow Tonya to take charge of the patient. "It's good to have someone here who knows what to do."

"It looks to me like you did well. You may have kept this man from bleeding to death," she told Charley with obvious admiration for his actions. "You probably saved his life."

One of the EMTs handed Charley a jacket. He had not noticed the cold while he attended to the needs of the hurt man, but sudden he was shivering and was glad to have any garment to cover his upper body.

Charley stood away from the patient for a while and watched Tonya do her job. He was impressed with her take charge nature and complete devotion to the task at hand. *There's a lady who understands the importance of her work, and knows how to get it done*, he told himself. *And besides that, she's beautiful*. He hoped for a moment with her before she left the scene, but that didn't happen as the devoted young lady never left the side of the crash victim.

The day was almost gone by the time Charley got back to Adairsville. When he got home, he made his way to the bedroom closet to find a shirt. He decided the color didn't matter much since just about any shade would complement the khakis he had on. He chose a solid blue one which he put on and tucked into his pants. *I could improve my wardrobe considerably if I take that job,* he decided as he looked around him at the apartment where he had lived for the past three years, *and I could certainly live in a place better than this dump. I need to talk with Davis.*

Charley knew that Davis would have closed his bookshop by now and probably be home. He thought about a visit, but he decided he didn't want to interrupt the little time the newlyweds had to spend with each other. He thought about Tonya. Maybe he could call her just to talk, but he remembered that she would still be on duty. *I don't know if I can stand another night of sitting here alone staring at those four walls. There's always the bar,* he thought, *the place where everybody knows your name. I could find someone to keep me company there. I guess I'll see if I can find a program worth watching on TV. I can't get in trouble with that.* The happy go-lucky man-about-town Charley Nelson settled in for another long night. He envied his friend Davis Morgan. *He's got just about all a man could want.* Charley sat down in front of his TV, and opened the folder Jim Lipscomb had given him.

CHAPTER 6

Davis loved piddling around in his shop. He sat in a chair with several books stacked in front of him, and one open in his right hand. He didn't see Charley until he heard his voice.

"I wish I had time to sit around and read," Charley teased.

"Even if you had the time, you wouldn't read," Davis replied. "When was the last time you read a book?"

"I think it was in senior English when I had to do a book report," Charley told his friend. "I've considered taking up reading again, but I don't know where to start. Why don't you pick out a book for me?" he suggested.

"I would love to do that. What kinds of stories do you...?"

"Wait a minute," Charley interrupted. "There's no way I'll pay you for one of your high-priced books. I just want to *borrow* one."

"Well, Charley, you should know this isn't a lending library, but because this is such a stretch for you, I'll lend you an inexpensive copy of a good book. Notice I said an *inexpensive copy*. There's no way I'll let you walk out of here with any book with real value. What about this one?" Davis strode over to pull a brown covered book off one of the shelves. "Do you think you might like a western? In my opinion, Louis L'Amour is heads and shoulders above any of the other western fiction writers. Why don't you give this one a try? It's called *Mustang Man*. I haven't read it, but I've liked every book I've ever read by L'Amour," Davis told him, and handed him the brown vinyl covered book.

"I'll give it a try," Charley told him.

Charley must be really bored, Davis decided. *Three months ago, to read a book would've been out of the question.*

"Since I'm officially on duty, I have only a moment, but I want to run something by you." Charley spoke quietly as he looked around. "Yesterday, I met with a man named Jim Lipscomb."

Davis knew he was supposed to know who that was, but for the life of him, he couldn't put a person to the name.

Charley who probably noticed the puzzled expression on Davis's face explained. "He's the gentlemen who so graciously forgave Ted Mason."

Davis then immediately recalled who Lipscomb was. Though he had never met the man, he was extremely impressed with what he had heard of him. Caught up in a gambling addiction, Ted had stolen a considerable amount of money from his employer. Rather than send him to prison, Lipscomb laid down some requirements for the young man, and offered to help him if he would meet those conditions. "Yes, I remember," Davis stated. "But why did you meet with him?"

"To make a long story short," Charley answered, "He needs a pilot and someone to help with security. Ted told him about me. He had me checked out, and offered me a job that would triple my present salary, improve my insurance situation considerably, and give me a great pension. The problem is I would have to move to Savannah, and, as much as I like to fly, I don't know if I want to give up police work. I've dreamed, for a while, of someday being chief here as my father once was, but even the chief's position in our little town wouldn't provide for me what I could have if I do accept Mr. Lipscomb's offer. That's it in a nutshell, and I guess I'm here to ask you to help me make that decision."

For a moment, Davis stood in silence. He could not fathom life in Adairsville without his close friend who had been his most constant companion since he returned to his hometown from Indianapolis. He and Charley had been through a lot together, and besides that, he knew if Charley moved to Savannah, his chance to reach the young man for the Lord would be greatly diminished. Yet, how could he suggest to Charley that he turn down such an opportunity? *That would be pure selfishness on my part,* Davis decided. He tried to get a handle on what Charley had just slapped him with before he responded.

When he finally spoke, the stunned Davis could only say to his friend, "Charley, I'll not tell you what to do, but I will say to you, be careful. Happiness is not determined by what one has. I value your friendship greatly, and I can't imagine you not being around. However, I know that is selfishness on my part and you need to do what works best for you. If you decide to accept the job and move to Savannah, if that will make you happy, then do it. If staying here works best for you, then that is what you need to do. It goes without saying that I'll pray for you as you make that decision, and I'll support you, whichever way you decide to go."

"I hope you'll do that. I have a month to decide. We'll talk about it some more when I have more time," Charley turned to hurry out of the shop. He took a few steps before he turned to say to Davis, "This is just between the two of us, okay?"

"Okay, it's just between you and me," Davis told him.

"What's with Romeo?" Janie asked a few moments after Charley exited. "He walked right past me and didn't even stop to flirt with me. I must've lost my looks and charm," she told Davis.

"You've lost none of your beauty or charm, Janie. Charley just has something on his mind." *And, undoubtedly, it'll be heavy on my mind for a time.* After Janie left his corner, Davis bowed his head to silently pray for his friend.

Davis ate lunch at Maggie Mae's Tea Room, located next to his shop. As he almost always did when he had lunch there, he ordered the chicken salad, but pondering the possibility of Charley's active friendship not being a part of his daily life spoiled his appetite He enjoyed the meal far less than usual. He got up from his table when he saw a well-dressed gentleman go into his shop. "Can I help you sir?" he asked the middle-aged gentleman.

"I'm Bertram Shaw," he announced to Davis. "I live up the road a few miles and recently, I learned about Corra Harris and I have developed a real interest in her. Since you named your shop for her, I thought you might have material about her or by her."

"Sure, I do," Davis told him. "It couldn't be the Corra Harris Bookshop if we didn't have books by her in our stock. I have a couple of copies of John Talmadge's biography of her entitled, *Lady of Purpose*. Of course, I have several reprint softcover copies of *A Circuit Rider's Wife*. I also have two original hardcover editions of that title."

"Are those first editions?" Shaw asked.

"No, I'm sure they aren't," Davis answered. "The true first would be found in one of the early twentieth century magazines. Most of Mrs. Harris's books were first published as serials in those periodicals," Davis told him. "These are early editions, but there is no way to determine if they were part of the earliest book printings. That would be true of the other titles I have here as well. I also have *The Recording Angel*, *The Co-Citizen* and *The Eyes of Love*." Davis spent the better part of an hour to answer Mr. Shaw's questions about the life and work of this local author who seemed to be regaining some notoriety among the local crowd. The time was well used, however, since Mr. Shaw left only after he put more than one hundred fifty dollars for Harris material on his Visa card.

* * *

It was well into the afternoon when Davis arrived at the Floyd Medical Center to visit with Bessie Taylor. He was glad to learn she had been taken from ICU to a room on the third floor. "I'm scheduled to be released tomorrow. My daughter, Penny and son, Peter, who both live in Carrollton, will stay with me alternately over the next few weeks. The two of them will remain with me for a week at a time until it's safe for me to be home alone," Bessie told him.

Davis wondered if it would ever be safe for Bessie to again live alone. He silently questioned if anyone had told her about Ole Sam. "I'm glad you're well enough to be released. And I'm glad you'll have some time with your son and daughter."

"I look forward to it. I've not seen them often in recent years," she told Davis.

"By the way," Davis said, when he pulled the little spoon he had found on the floor of his storage closet out of his pocket, "Was this in the box you gave me?"

"Yes, it was," Bessie said after she squinted to get a good look at the item. "That spoon once belonged to Corra Harris. I used to have lots of items that belonged to her - objects she gave me, but most of those have been lost or somehow slipped away through the years. That spoon was in a box of odds and ends from her estate that I bought at an auction at the depot, maybe thirty years back. I knew of your interest in her, and thought you might like to have it. When I'm gone, I want you to have the few other goodies I still have from Mrs. Harris's estate plus a few other odds and ends I think you would enjoy."

"You're indeed a thoughtful person Bessie, but are you sure you want to part with this spoon? Wouldn't you like to keep it?"

"I'm an old lady who will soon be with the Lord. I'll have no use for it then," Bessie told him. "I'd rather you had it than it be innocently discarded when I'm gone."

"Thank you, Bessie. You're a generous lady. I assure you I will treasure it, and like you, I will someday pass it on to someone who will appreciate its significance," Davis told the gracious lady in the hospital bed.

The two talked for a few more minutes, not so much as preacher and parishioner, but as two friends. Davis took her hand to pray with her before he left. He exited the room, as he often did, after he visited with someone Bessie's age, wondering if perhaps this would be the last time he would see her in this world.

* * *

Amy despised being alone at night, but she knew the more time Jay spent out at the house in Folsom, the quicker they could move in and spend their time together. She did not even see him before he left today. Atlanta traffic must have been lighter than usual because he got home early, while she had a parent conference that kept her at school later than she ordinarily would have been there. She hoped he remembered to take a couple of sandwiches with him. At times such as this, she almost regretted they decided to purchase the fixer-upper out in the country, but then when she considered what they would have after the job was finished, she knew they made the right decision. *Oh well*, she thought, *I would've had to grade these papers even if Jay were here.*

When alone in the house, Amy heard almost every sound around her. She listened closely when she thought she heard steps on her back porch. There were no further noises, but she decided to investigate anyway. She got up from the sofa and made her way to the window in the kitchen that allowed her to look out over the back porch. Just as she got close enough to see outside, she looked directly into the eyes of a head that popped up on the other side of the window. What she saw left her completely speechless for a moment. It was a face decorated with white clown make-up, with red lips and black around the eyes. The head was covered with a black hood. Startled, Amy instinctively stepped back and threw her hands above her head before she screamed with deafening volume, "It's the Creeper! It's the Adairsville Creeper!"

CHAPTER 7

E ven through the clown make-up, Amy could see the figure outside her window was as startled as she was. She sprinted to the corner where she grabbed her broom before she exited through the doorway and yelled, "I'll show you what we do to creepers around here!"

The lanky figure dressed in jeans and a black sweatshirt turned to run and almost fell to the ground when he jumped off the porch. He hobbled, evidently having hurt his ankle, yet he continued to run fast enough to stay ahead of the English teacher with her broom. Amy chased him through her neighbor's yard and across Park Street. He still limped a bit, but despite that he increased the distance between himself and Amy and her broom. Then he went across the Christian Church parking lot and turned left onto Hotel Street. Amy now out of breath stopped and cried out, "You show up around here again and you'll have to pick splinters out of your head!" He was soon out of sight.

Several neighbors who heard the commotion were now assembled on the church parking lot. "What's this all about?" Mr. Allison, whose yard Amy had just dashed through, asked in a rather agitated voice.

"Oh, some nut in a black hoodie and a clown face peeped through my window," Amy answered.

"That's the Creeper!" a lady with a cell phone in her hand shrieked. "I'll call the police," she offered.

In a matter of minutes ten or twelve people were assembled in the spacious lot, along with two of Adairsville's finest. Amy answered the policemen's questions while her neighbors listened.

"There was something familiar about him," she told one of the officers. "I'm not sure what it was, maybe the eyes, or the way he ran.... I'm not sure what it was, but there was something about him that caused me to think I had seen him before."

"How tall would you say he is?" the officer asked.

"I don't know, maybe six feet or six-one. I didn't have time to measure him."

"Was he old or young?" the other officer asked.

"I suspect he was fairly young. I think he hurt his ankle when he jumped off the porch, and he still outran me, and I can pick them up and put them down pretty well," the young teacher, who was a dedicated jogger, added.

"We'll keep an eye on your house," one of the policemen told her before they got into their patrol car to leave.

"I'd appreciate it," Amy responded. "But please don't come around to the window at the back of the house," she said with a giggle.

"No, Ma'am, we know better than that," the policeman said as he eyed the broom Amy still held in her hand.

Amy walked back to her house escorted by Mr. Allison. She found her cell phone, which she had left on the sofa before all the excitement, to call Jay. His response was predictable, "I'll be home as soon as I can get there. Have you called your dad?" he asked.

"No, I won't call him tonight. He doesn't need the worry." She was tempted to tell him she was fine, so he could go ahead and finish his work at the house, but she didn't because she decided it would be good to have him home a little early tonight.

* * *

It wasn't until the next day when his wife came home from school with the story that Davis learned of his daughter's adventure the previous night. He immediately called her and asked,

"Why didn't you call us when all of your excitement was taking place last night?"

"There was no reason for me to do that," his daughter told him. "It was no big deal, and I didn't want to bother you."

"No big deal!" Davis raised his voice. "You came face to face with the Adairsville Creeper and you say it was no big deal."

"I'm sure it was just a prank. I don't think he intended to hurt me."

"You can't assume that! To presume a prowler will not hurt you could cost you your life. Wake up Amy! I had hoped you would've learned by now that not everyone in this world is a good person."

"I know that, Dad, but haven't you always taught me that it's right to presume the best about a person instead of the worst?"

"Yes, Honey, but I wasn't talking about the Adairsville Creeper. Use your head. Practice a little caution."

"The Adairsville Creeper is probably some kid who thinks he's funny," Amy replied. "Don't worry Dad, I'll be careful and I promise you I'll keep you informed about out of the ordinary occurrences."

After he put his phone back into his pocket Davis told Deidre, "I love that girl with all my heart, but sometimes she infuriates me."

"I know," Deidre replied. "Don't forget that she was my roommate for a year. There's not a more lovable person anywhere, but she's no longer a girl. She's a woman, and the fact is your daughter is her own person. Nobody tells Amy what to do, but you know what? That's part of her charm. That's one of the characteristics that make her special."

"I suppose so," Davis responded, not totally convinced.

For a couple of minutes Deidre walked about their living room to move some small objects, while Davis sat with Amy on his mind. "I learned today that Barbara plans to go to South Georgia this weekend to visit with one of her sons, and Randi will be left all alone with no ballgame tomorrow night," Deidre broke the silence. "It might be a good time to get her and Charley together, if Charley isn't on duty."

"I'm fairly certain he has the evening off," Davis answered. "But I don't know that it would be such a good time for that. In fact, I don't know that them together as a couple is a good idea at all."

"What's the matter, Honey? Do you think Randi might corrupt your friend?" Deidre asked with a smile.

"It's not that exactly, but I happen to know Charley has some important matters on his mind right now. He's a bit preoccupied,"

"Maybe dinner in the company of an attractive young lady is just what he needs," Deidre suggested.

"Perhaps you're right," Davis reluctantly gave in. "I'll give him a call and ask him to have dinner with us tomorrow evening, but I'll not blindside him. I'll tell him that Randi will be here as well."

"I agree, and I will invite Randi, and inform her Charley will be present," Deidre told him. "We need to be completely upfront with both."

* * *

"Where've you been?" the voice on the other end of the line asked the young man with the scar on his cheek. "I've heard nothing from you since you searched that storage closet. Did you find it?"

"No, I didn't. I looked closely at all the junk in that stupid closet, and it wasn't there. I thought it best for me to get out of town for a day or two. I don't want to end up behind bars again."

"You've been to Atlanta to drink again, haven't you?" the voice accused. "I need for you to stay sober. I don't care what you do after we finish the job, but I need for you to stay functional until then. Don't let me down, and I'll make it worth your while. Are you at the same motel as before?"

"I'm at the same motel, but in a different room. I'm now in room twelve," the young man reported.

"I'll be back in touch with you. I need to do a little detective work, and then I'll give you your instructions. Keep that cell phone I gave you on and handy at all times," the voice demanded before hanging up.

After he laid down the phone the young man with the scar turned on the TV set and picked up the bottle he had brought back with him from Atlanta. *I'll finish this bottle and then I can sleep it off,* he told himself before he flopped back into the chair.

* * *

Friday was a busy day for Davis at the Corra Harris Bookshop, and that made Davis happy. He needed the business. Bertram Shaw, the gentlemen who recently became intrigued with Corra Harris came by, and that meant another sale and more questions directed to Davis about the writer. In late morning, a tour bus arrived, which brought more than thirty elderly people to the 1902 Stock Exchange. Several of them spent most of their time in the bookshop before they ate lunch at the Tea Room. Many returned to the bus with books in hand. It never ceased to amaze Davis that many of his vintage children's books were sold to people beyond retirement age. It took him a while, but he finally figured it out. They could not resist the books that had made a big impression on them as children, especially when they were editions that appeared exactly as they remembered.

Early afternoon, George Black, one of the deacons from the church, came in, not because he was interested in books, but because he needed some input from his interim pastor. "You know Tommy, my son, don't you? He's seldom in church anymore, but I figured you would remember him."

"Certainly, I remember him. I think I recall that he was a talented baseball player when he was in high school," Davis remarked.

"He was that – a mighty good shortstop," George responded with obvious pride. "Before he hurt his knee late in his senior year, several professional teams showed interest in drafting him. I guess it was when he lost that opportunity that he kind of quit on life. He hasn't been the same since. It's been more than two years since he graduated. He can't hold a job, and lately it's been booze. Almost every time I see him, he's all liquored up. I don't know what to do, Davis. I try to talk with him, but it goes in one ear and out the other. He's just gotten worse."

"I'm sorry to hear that, George. Do you have any suggestions about what I might do to help him?" Davis asked.

"I thought you might talk with him, Preacher," George said and looked a little sheepish. "I've made every argument I know to make. He won't listen to me. Maybe he'll pay attention to you."

"I'll do what I can to help, George, but to walk up to him and preach a sermon will do more harm than good. We need to open a door rather than build a wall. Give me some time to earn the right to be heard. He might be responsive if I can first create a rapport. I promise you, George, I'll work on it. Just give me a little time."

"You know what's best," George offered. The two friends sat and talked about church matters for a while before George got up to leave and extended his hand. "Thanks, preacher," he said.

"Thanks for your visit, George. Before you leave, could we take a moment to pray for Tommy?"

"You mean here and now?" the deacon responded and looked around him, obviously surprised at the suggestion.

"I don't see why not," Davis calmly responded with a grin. "The Lord's always ready to listen." With George's right hand still in his, Davis begin to pray, "Lord, you know Tommy better than we do, and you know what's in his heart...."

CHAPTER 8

D avis greeted his wife with a smile and a kiss when he got home from the shop on Friday. "There's a small matter of which I need to take care before I forget," he told Deidre. He went into the hallway and then to the small storage closet. Obviously, he hoped to find some object buried in the packed storage area. He moved stuff around, yet tried to keep them in reasonable order.

"What do you hope to find?" Deidre asked.

"I think I've found them," he announced when he pulled out first a fielder's glove and then a catcher's mitt which had a baseball in its pocket. Then when he reached into the corner of the closet to retrieve his wooden baseball bat, he saw the smile on Deidre's face instantly transformed to a look of terror. Then he saw that her eyes were focused on the baseball bat, and he suddenly realized exactly what was on her mind. "No Honey, it's not like that." Davis dropped all the objects in his hands to run to his bride and embrace her. "I promise you, this isn't like what happened with the Rat-Faced man or the Angry Indian who turned out not to be an Indian at all." Davis knew Deidre remembered the part the baseball bat played in those battles. It's not like that," he assured her. "These are tools I hope to use to help a wayward young man. It's not a weapon this time, just a *baseball* bat."

"You have no idea how seeing that bat scared me. I don't want you to ever put yourself in a position like that again," she told him.

"Didn't I promise you I would never again intentionally place myself in a situation that would be potentially dangerous?"

"I know you said that, and I believe you mean it, but it seems that those situations just naturally pop up wherever you happen to be. I just don't want you to get hurt," Deidre said almost in tears.

"Don't worry: I'm so cautious my friends call me *chicken*. Yesterday someone clucked when I walked by."

"You don't have to go that far," Deidre said with a giggle as she stepped back. "I don't want my husband to be a coward. Just be prudent."

"I can do that," Davis said before he took the baseball equipment to his Jeep where he placed it in the back. When he returned, Deidre was busy in the kitchen with the meal they would share with Randi and Charley. Every day Davis closed out his quiet time with at least one of the Psalms. This morning he had read Psalm 143 and one verse from that chapter popped in and out of his mind all day. He sat down in his recliner, picked up his Bible and turned to verse ten of that chapter. He read it again, *"Teach me to do your will, for you are my God; may your good Spirit lead me on level ground."*

That's what we want for this life, he decided. *We're looking for level ground – safe ground – ground without a lot of bumps and holes. Maybe not completely smooth, not necessarily beautifully paved, but never-the-less level-without destructive danger. And we're told the way to such a life is to be responsive to God's Holy Spirit. The Spirit we receive when we give our lives to the Lord is the way to attain safety on that level ground.*

Davis's sermon for Sunday about hypocrisy had been ready since Wednesday, but he knew it had to be pushed back to another day. His sermon Sunday would be, *The Safety of Walking on Level Ground.*

There was a knock on the door in the hallway. Davis knew that had to be Randi from the apartment next door. He placed his Bible on the little table beside his chair and rose to go to the door. "Good evening, Randi. We're pleased you could join us tonight."

"Thank you for the invitation. I wasn't excited about dinner alone tonight," the tall and tanned blond girl told him.

She's almost as tall as Charley; he told himself when he remembered that Charley was at least two inches shorter than his own six-foot frame. "I can't imagine that the young men of our town would allow you to spend an evening alone."

"So far, I haven't found one I'm interested in spending time with," Randi told Davis, and looked away from him. "It's not that there haven't been invitations."

Deidre came into the room from the kitchen. "Hi Randi. How did basketball practice go today?"

"It was a typical practice. So far, it's been a long season, and I don't see that it'll get much better anytime soon. Our girls are young and still have a long way to go," the coach responded.

"I'm sure they will be fine when they get a little experience under their belts," Davis added.

"I hope so, but I would just as soon not talk about basketball, if it's okay with you," Randi informed them.

"That's fine with me," Davis told her. "Tell me, what would you like to talk about?"

"I'm interested in your bookshop. How long have you been in the collectable book business?" Randi asked.

"I've been into books for a long time, but it's been just over a year since I left Indianapolis to come home to live and open the shop. A lot of water has gone under the bridge in that year," Davis added, and turned toward his wife with a grin. "There hasn't been a dull moment."

"Really?" Randi seemed surprised. "Where do you find the excitement?"

"Oh, we don't look for it, it just comes to us," Davis answered before he heard the doorbell ring. "That's got to be Charley." Davis got up to go to the front door.

"Come on in Charley. Randi's already here," Davis told him. Charley followed Davis into the front room. "Randi, this is the legendary Charley Nelson, of whom I am sure you have heard of, and perhaps been warned about. Charley, this is Randi Metcalf, our girls' basketball coach who doesn't want to talk about basketball."

"I'm glad she doesn't want to talk basketball, because there are other matters I'd rather talk with her about," Charley said with his eyes feasting on the beautiful young woman on the sofa. "I'm pleased to finally meet you, Randi. The more correct word than the one Davis used to describe me is probably *infamous*. And if you have heard anything about me, I hope you will forget it all. I'm sure most of it's not true," Charley told her.

"I'm pleased to meet you and I would be disappointed if it weren't true," Randi replied, with her mouth curved into a smile.

"Dinner will be ready in a few minutes. Why don't we sit down and get to know one another?" Deidre suggested. She seated herself in one of the chairs in the room while Charley sat down on the sofa beside Randi and Davis went back to his recliner.

"I understand you're a police officer," Randi said to Charley. "I suppose, in a town like Adairsville, you spend most of your time writing traffic tickets and helping school children cross the street."

"Sure, like police officers in most places, I do a lot of that, but there are times when we get involved in some pretty heavy stuff," Charley told her.

"I can't imagine that," Randi countered. "Adairsville seems so quiet and uncomplicated."

"Most of the time that's true, but we have our share of drugs, violence, and crime," Charley said. "For example, just recently my aunt's watchdog was poisoned and someone broke into her home and slugged her before he tore the house apart, evidently looking for something."

"Did the lab determine the dog was definitely poisoned?" Davis asked.

"No doubt about it! The autopsy revealed meat in the dog's stomach, laced with poison - enough to kill a horse," Charley added.

"Then Bessie Taylor is your aunt," Randi surmised. "I didn't realize that. How is she?"

"She seems to be slow to get back on her feet, but I guess you would expect that of someone who is ninety-two years old," Charley answered.

"Is it true that she actually met Margaret Mitchell? I'm fascinated with Margaret Mitchell and everything about *Gone with the Wind*," Randi admitted to him.

"Yes, it's true. Aunt Bessie, as a child was a friend and often companion of Corra Harris and due to that friendship met a good many famous people."

"Wow, I would like to talk with her about that some time," Randi replied, with her face aglow.

"I tell you what, when Aunt Bessie gets better, I'll take you out to meet her and you can ask her whatever questions you want. She would enjoy your company." Charley told her.

"Would you do that? I would love that." Randi told him. "I would forever be in your debt. Just to meet someone who knew Margaret Mitchell would be a thrill for me."

Deidre got up from her chair. "It should be just about ready," she told them while she walked toward the kitchen. She returned after a few moments to ask, "Are you ready to eat? It's on the table." They went into the big country kitchen, which also served as a dining room and sat down around the table before Davis asked the Lord to bless the meal.

"Tell me, Charley, do you know Tommy Black?" Davis asked as the food was passed.

"Yes, I know him. He's George's boy, isn't he?"

"That's right. Has he been in any serious trouble?" Davis questioned.

"No, not any serious trouble. We've locked him up overnight three or four times. As I remember, he doesn't seem to be able to hold his liquor, and from time to time we've found him passed out somewhere around town, usually in a parked car."

"Why do you ask?" Charley inquired.

"His dad came to me today, and asked for my help with the boy. I just wondered what I was up against," Davis stated.

"He's certainly a boy worth salvaging," Charley said. "That boy was one of the best high school baseball players we've had in this town."

When Deidre heard that, she turned toward her husband with a twinkle in her eyes and caught his attention to silently mouth the words, *I love you!*

Davis understood exactly what that was about and returned the smile of his wife. When much of the food was consumed and an abundance of conversation had passed among the four people, Randi turned toward Davis, "You're the one with the literary expertise, let me ask you a question. I've heard there are a couple of lost Margaret Mitchell manuscripts that may or may not have survived somewhere out there. What do you think about that? Is it true?"

This girl has Margaret Mitchell on the brain, Davis decided. *That obsession probably won't endear her to Charley.* He could see that Charley looked a little bored with the literary references.

"I've heard and read that, but I don't know if it's true," Davis answered. "I'm sure you know that a few years ago her early manuscript *Lost Laysen,* which she had given to an old boyfriend, was discovered in a shoe box along with some love letters and photographs. While it wasn't exactly *Gone with the Wind,* it made someone a lot of money. I've heard that as a teenager, Mitchell wrote a four-hundred-page story entitled *The Big Four.* about girls in a boarding school. I've also heard she wrote a novelette in the nineteen twenties that was submitted to a publisher, but turned down because it was too short. That is rather ironic when you consider the length of *Gone with the Wind*. I suspect anyone who found his or herself in procession of either of those manuscripts would be fixed for life."

Randi left first. "I'd love to see you in church Sunday," Davis told Charley a few minutes later as he was on his way out. "I think the sermon I have planned for that day would be helpful to you."

"Maybe I'll be there," Charley replied. "It couldn't do me any harm. Incidentally," he added, "You need to pick me out another book. I enjoyed that western you gave me."

Who would have thought? If that change can occur, others can too. Davis and Deidre talked for a time after their guests left before they retired for the night. It occurred to Davis that not long ago, he considered himself no less than Job's cousin – an afflicted man – now his thoughts were, *I'm a man who is blessed, indeed.*

CHAPTER 9

Davis went to the church office after breakfast on Saturday. Since he changed his sermon mid-stream, he needed to give the new idea some structure. He learned a long time ago that it's not enough to have a word to say. How those ideas are presented is of extreme importance if they are to be heard, and hopefully implemented. In deep thought with his computer screen in front of him and Bible open beside him, he almost didn't hear the knock on the study door. He got out of his desk chair and walked the five or six steps to open the door. He didn't recognize the man who stood in front of him, perhaps thirty to thirty-five years of age, with unkempt brown hair.

"Are you Pastor Morgan?" the man asked with a high-pitched voice with so little volume that Davis had to listen closely to comprehend his words.

"Yes, I'm Davis Morgan." Davis held his right hand out to shake the hand of the gentleman who had a rather sour look on his face. "What can I do for you?" Davis asked with a friendly grin.

"I am P.W. Taylor, Bessie Taylor's grandson. I guess you know Grandma Bessie isn't well after that fall. We don't think she'll make it. She could die at any time."

Davis was surprised at the crude and seemingly unconcerned way the grandson evaluated his grandmother's condition, and he didn't agree that it was a *fall* that was responsible for her physical state. Davis was sure she'd received a blow to the head from behind, but he didn't offer the man his opinion.

"We know you've gone to see Grandma Bessie a couple of times recently, and Dad once heard her say she wanted you to have some of her stuff when she was gone. The family wondered if she might have given you the key to her storage bin out near the hardware store north of town? We need that key to retrieve some items she stored there."

"She did tell me there were some special objects of common interest that she would like me to have when the time came, but she gave me no key," Davis assured his inquisitive visitor.

"Should she give you that key, you need to pass it on to me. The items stored in that bin are important to the family," P.W. Taylor told him in a tone that sounded like an order.

"Bessie is a dear friend of mine, and I'll honor her wishes. I don't expect that she will give me any keys, but should that happen, I'll do with them whatever she requests," Davis countered.

"You would do well to do what I instructed you to do," P.W. said with a smirk before he turned to leave the room. When he got to the door, he twirled to glare at Davis for a moment before he warned, "We'll do whatever we have to do to keep you away from what is rightfully ours."

"I assure you, Mr. Taylor, that I don't want any part of whatever is rightfully yours," Davis asserted before the man stomped away.

I wonder what that's all about, Davis asked himself. *Bessie is a grand lady who has in some ways lived an enchanted life, but I can't imagine that she has any valuables that would stir-up such aggression.*

Davis took his cell phone from the top of his desk after which he selected the correct number and held it to his ear. "Charley, I just had an unusual visit from one of your cousins, a rather disagreeable chap by the name of P.W. Taylor."

"What did *Petey* want? We seldom see him sober enough to put two words together. I hope he didn't give you a hard time."

"No, not really. His visit was relatively brief. He wanted to know if Bessie had given me a key to her storage bin. He made it clear that, should I receive that key, I needed to get it to him immediately. It's obvious that he resents Bessie's intention to give me a few token items from her estate."

"Don't pay him any mind. Petey, like his dad, is out to get whatever he can get out of life without investing any real work. Neither father nor son has ever been much interested in Aunt Bessie unless there was some reward for them. I have the key which Petey wants. Aunt Bessie gave it to me, and asked me to keep it until she was gone. She said I was then to open the bin and distribute what is there in accordance with how it is tagged. She did indicate to me that there are some treasures there for you," Charley told him.

"I don't want to be the source of any problems for your family," Davis told his friend. "You do whatever you think best in regard to any object or box with my name on it."

"Bessie asked me to be the executor of her estate, and I plan to see her wishes executed exactly as she has instructed," Charley responded. "Incidentally, you'll be happy to know that I have a date with Randi tonight. I'm not sure if it is my charm and good looks that attracted her or the fact that my aunt briefly knew Margaret Mitchell, but never-the-less she is interested, and I've never been one to shy away from a beautiful woman who shows interest in me."

"Well, behave yourself and have a good time," Davis told him.

"You can be sure I'll not get out of line with your friend," Charley assured him, and then there was silence. Charley was gone. Davis was always a bit annoyed by Charley's abrupt conclusions to telephone conversations, but he had grown to expect it.

* * *

It was one of those night shifts in which little of significance had happened. That was good and that was bad. No activity meant there were no emergencies – nobody had been injured or hurt, but it also meant the night could get long and boring. When you worked Emergency Medical Services for Bartow County, you moved around among the five stations. Tonya Willis spent most of her time at the Cassville site, but tonight found herself out on Highway 140 in Adairsville. She could hear the chatter of her companions in the station, but since she was almost asleep, their voices seemed to come from a distance. She was aroused from her slumber by one of her co-workers who called out, "Wake up Tonya; it's barely past eight o'clock."

"You remind me of my three-year-old niece," she told Bob, her partner for the night, who seemed to have some bias against catching a few winks when possible. "Anytime I doze off around her, she gets in my face and yells 'boo!'"

"Would you like to have a cup of coffee?" Bob asked her.

"No, I had my two-cup quota for the evening with that slice of cake I had for dinner, but I do appreciate your kindness – your offer to serve me."

"Serve you! That's not what I had in mind. I was about to suggest you retrieve a cup for each of us."

"You know better than that. I didn't become an EMT to do kitchen duty or to be a waitress," Tonya, who was born the lone female among five siblings, said with a half-smile. The good-natured banter continued for a few minutes until the call came. There was an accident on I-75 at the south bound ramp.

In a matter of seconds, they were in gear and headed in that direction, lights were flashing and siren blaring. Bob was behind the wheel, and since sometimes a swift arrival was critical, he was evidently determined to get to the scene as fast as possible. As they swiftly progressed toward their destination, without warning, a lumber truck seemed to come out of nowhere and headed straight toward them. Bob swerved to avoid a head-on crash, but the truck plowed, with major impact, into the passenger side of the emergency vehicle. The last memory Tonya had before she lost consciousness was the sensation of rolling over and over.

It was a half-hour later before she had any further idea of what had happened. When she came to, she was in the back of another ambulance, this time on a stretcher headed for the Floyd Emergency Center with an attendant beside her. She began to take inventory. Her right arm seemed to be okay, but she could not lift her left one. She also felt pain in her left leg and tried without success to lift it. Her own diagnosis of her condition was a broken left arm and leg. She pondered the possibility of internal injuries. Her thoughts went to Bob and then to the accident on the ramp. The compassionate emergency responder wondered how those victims had made out, but when she tried to question the attendant in charge, she could get no intelligible words to come out of her mouth. Her attempt to communicate produced only grunts. Her thoughts were muddled and Tonya became frustrated with her inability to function. Then it all went black again.

* * *

Davis and Deidre had enjoyed a quiet evening at home. As they prepared to retire at about ten-thirty, Davis's cell phone rang. "Hello, Davis. I don't like to be the bearer of bad news, but I thought you needed to know that Aunt Bessie passed away earlier tonight."

"I'm sorry, Charley. That's, no doubt, bad news for us, but it's good news for her. She's gone to be with the Lord. Are there family members at her home?" Davis asked.

"I believe both Pete and Penny are there along with Petey. I don't know whether any of the other grandchildren have gotten there yet. There is another matter I want you to pray about," Charley continued. "Do you remember Tonya Willis?"

"Yes, I do. She is the attractive EMT, isn't she?"

"That's right; she was the lady who responded to Aunt Bessie's emergency. A colleague called me while I was at dinner with Randi to tell me that Tonya and her partner Bob Jenson were hit by a truck when they responded to an accident. Bob is banged up, but seemed to come through it with no serious injuries, Tonya didn't fare as well. I don't know the extent of her injuries, but I'm told it doesn't look good. I think I'll go to Floyd Medical Center to check on her. It won't do me much good to stay here. I won't be able to sleep."

"I'll pray for her full recovery. You be careful on your trip to and from Rome."

Davis knew the obituary would state that Bessie had died of natural causes, but he recognized his friend's life had been cut short by the blow she had taken to her head. That disturbed him and perhaps made him a little angry. He had hoped to get a good night's rest with all the Sunday activities just ahead, but he knew it was his duty to touch base with Bessie's family. In a few moments, he had gotten out of his pajamas and back into the clothes he had discarded earlier and was on his way to the Pine Log area. When he recalled P. W's visit earlier that day, he wondered how he would be received; nevertheless, he owed it to Bessie to do what he could to comfort her family.

While he drove along Summer Street, Davis caught a glimpse of someone darting across the road beside the Baptist Church and up the hill toward the old funeral home. It took him a split second to realize that person wore what appeared to be a black hoodie. He slammed on his brakes, but the figure was out of sight immediately. Davis turned his car around and raced back down the hill and turned right on the Old Dixie Highway. He stopped in front of the old Masonic Lodge, got out of his car, but was unable to spot the suspicious figure he had seen earlier. He reluctantly got back into his car and continued his trip to Bessie's house.

Pete and Penny, Bessie's son and daughter were at the house when Davis arrived. P.W. came in after he had been there for fifteen minutes. Pete and P.W. said little to him, and their stiff body language told him they resented his presence there. Penny seemed genuinely pleased with his attempt to minister to the family. Before he left, Penny told him, "Preacher, you know we want you to conduct the service. Mama loved you and would want no one else to oversee her *send off*. We will probably meet with the funeral director tomorrow or first thing Monday. I don't know for sure, but we hope we can have the funeral Tuesday. We'll let you know when the arrangements are firm."

"I would count it an honor to preside at Bessie's memorial. She was one of my favorite people, you know." Davis asked the three family members present to join him in a circle. They joined hands, and he prayed for their peace in the loss of their loved one.

On the way home, Davis wondered about the condition of Tonya Willis as well as about her spiritual status. He silently prayed for Tonya and for Charley. He guessed that Charley was fonder of the girl than he let on. He could not help but speculate about where Charley was in relation to his crucial decision about his future. He prayed about that as well. Almost before he knew it, he had parked his red Jeep Wrangler in front of his house, but it was well past mid-night, and there was a sermon to be preached in the morning.

CHAPTER 10

Davis was pleasantly surprised when he looked over the congregation on Sunday. The three hundred seat assembly room was almost full. Good attendance is always a plus for any preacher. No one likes to preach to empty pews. But it wasn't the attendance count that pleased him most this day. He was delighted to see two people he had not expected as part of the crowd. Charley Nelson was on the end of the next to last pew with Randi Metcalf at his side. Randi had been a frequent visitor since she came to town, but Charley was seldom part of the Sunday congregation.

The other person whose presence thrilled Davis was his ninety-plus year-old friend and fellow local historian, Helen Townsend. She was seated toward the middle of the west side of the auditorium, and she smiled widely when their eyes met. Miss Helen, who normally could be found at the Methodist Church on Sunday, had taken it upon herself to convince Davis that he needed to be back in the ministry. She had scolded him more than once with passionate, scripture-filled lectures, for putting his hand to the plough and turning back. Davis knew she was pleased and, no doubt, counted it a personal victory to see him on the platform in charge of the service.

Early in the service Davis informed the people of the death of Bessie Taylor. "The arrangements are incomplete now, but will be on our website and that of the Barton Funeral Home as soon as they are complete." He also requested they join him to pray for the seriously injured Tonya Willis. "She is a special young lady – a first responder, who was hurt attempting to aid others," he told them.

Davis watched the congregation while he presented his *Level Ground* sermon based on Psalm 143:10, and observed by their attention that they were with him. *That's good*, he determined. *That probably means the message promises an answer to a perceived need.*

"Notice that *Spirit* in that verse is spelled with a capital S," the preacher suggested to his listeners. "That indicates this is a reference to God's Holy Spirit. The Holy Spirit in Old Testament times generally worked on the person from the outside. Today, under the New Covenant, He works from within, for we are told in Acts 2:38 that when we become Christians, we receive the *gift* of God's Spirit. God comes to live in us as we live our lives day by day. We who are in the Lord have all the help we need. Our part then is to acknowledge and accept the power that is within us."

Davis continued, "Sometimes we become frustrated when we try to make decisions for our lives." Davis saw Charley sit up straight and focus directly on him. "To be on firm ground - a place where it is comfortable for us to walk, we Christians need to seek God's *will*. When we walk with him, we are on level ground.

"So, how do we determine God's will after we have requested it be revealed to us? I propose that about ninety per cent of the time, that can be determined when we search the Word of God. God's Word is not so much a rule book as it is God's guide for our lives. But what about those times when we must decide about matters not clearly handled in the Bible, such as where does God want us or what job does God want us to accept? What then? Maybe that which I am about to suggest is an over simplification, but I don't think so. We would do well to pray and then wait. Pray some more and wait some more. If God has a preference, He will let you know in some way. And if you do not find clear direction, perhaps God doesn't have a preference. You are then free to go in the direction that makes you happy. It is imperative, however, that before you take that step on your own, that you give God full rein, and be ready to follow His guidance."

After the service people stepped out of the way to allow Miss Helen to immediately make her way to the preacher. "You're back behind the plough!" she declared while she vigorously shook his hand with her face beaming. "Back where you belong. Come by the house sometime soon and we'll talk and have a glass of sweet tea," she instructed. Before she let go of his right hand, she told him. "I was sorry to hear about Bessie. We were close to the same age, you know. I wasn't very well acquainted with her when we were children, her out in the country and me a town girl, but we became fast friends later in life. She had some great stories to tell."

Randi stood a few feet away when Charley greeted Davis. "Thanks, Pal, that was helpful, and thank you for the prayer for Tonya," he said quietly.

"How did you find her last night?" Davis inquired.

"I wasn't permitted to see her, but the news I got wasn't all bad. She has some broken bones; I think an arm and a leg. They were concerned about a possible concussion, and perhaps internal bleeding, but I was told she was conscious, though befuddled," Charley reported. "After Randi and I get some lunch, I will try again to see her."

"Would you like for me to go with you?" Davis asked his friend.

"I don't want to spoil your Sunday afternoon, but if you are free, I would love to have you come along. Maybe you could pray with her," Charley responded.

"Sure, I can do that. Deidre and I plan to go home for some lunch. I should be available after about two o'clock."

"I'll deliver Randi and pick you up around two or two thirty." Davis took note that Randi was listening to their conversation from a distance, and didn't seem to be pleased.

* * *

Davis and Charley left the house in Charley's Chevy before two-thirty on their way to Rome. Almost immediately, after they turned left onto Old Highway 41 or as it was once known, the Old Dixie Highway, they passed a figure that rapidly walked north. "That's Tommy Black, isn't it? Can we give him a ride? I need to talk with him." Davis spoke hurriedly before they got too far past the young man.

Charley stopped the car and it took the boy a moment to comprehend that they were stopped for him. When he got into the back seat of the car, Davis asked, "Where're you headed, Tommy?"

"I'm on my way to Bertram Shaw's house," Tommy told him. "It's about a mile and a half up the highway. He has a little work he wants me to do, but I wasn't excited about hoofing it that far."

"I know Mr. Shaw. He's the gentlemen who comes into my shop and is interested in Corra Harris books," Davis told their passenger.

"That's him, all right. He loves books. In fact, that's why I'm on my way out there. I'm to help him build some bookcases. I've been out of work for a while and odd jobs like this one helps see me through," Tommy told them.

When he noticed a Band-Aid on Tommy's right cheek, Charley asked him, "How did you injure your cheek?"

"I fell and cut it," the boy sheepishly replied. "I seem to trip over my own feet a lot these days."

"Tommy, as I remember, you are a fantastic baseball player. Maybe you could help me. I plan to play on the church softball team when spring comes. I played high school ball and summer baseball in Calhoun when I was a teen, but I haven't thrown or caught a ball in years. I need some practice before the season starts or they may decide they can't use the ole preacher. I'd hate to get cut by my own church. Maybe we could go over to Manning Mill Park and throw a few when we get a pretty day," Davis suggested.

"We can do that, Mr. Morgan." Tommy perked up. "I love to throw the baseball around."

"Then we'll do it." Davis said and smiled at the boy. "I'll call your dad and have him relay the message to you when I am available and the temperature is around the sixty-degree mark."

After they delivered the boy to the Shaw house, they headed back to Highway 140 and turned west toward Rome.

"You know that whoever hit Aunt Bessie killed her," Charley abruptly broke the silence. "I plan to use my off-duty time over the next few days to see if I can't bring that murderer to justice. If we catch the Adairsville Creeper we will also have Aunt Bessie's attacker."

"Maybe, but I don't have to tell you to be careful. And if there's any way I can help you, let me know. I loved Bessie too," Davis told him.

"Before I forget, let me fill you in on the call that came to the station last night between ten-thirty and eleven. Clark Landrum reported that someone who wore a black hoodie tried to pry open the gate at the storage facility near the hardware store. By the time our boys got there, he was gone. He did a number on the lock, but it would appear he didn't get inside. Sounds like another Creeper sighting," Charley added.

"I don't know," Davis spoke up. "I didn't report it, but when I left between ten-thirty and eleven o'clock last night to visit your aunt's family, I saw someone in a black hoodie on the hillside at the old vacant funeral home. I drove around to the other side, but he disappeared. It would be hard for him to be at two different places at the same time."

"It could be done in that thirty-minute span if he had a car," Charley suggested.

"I suppose it could, but I spotted no car. I think the guy I saw was on foot."

"Why didn't you report it?" Charley asked.

"I thought about it, but as far as I could see, he broke no law. To wear a black sweatshirt with a hood is no crime. I really didn't have anything to report."

"Maybe the guy you saw was an innocent kid who just happened to wear a black hoodie type shirt and the guy at the storage area was the real McCoy," Charley guessed.

"Or maybe it was the other way around. Maybe I saw the Creeper and the guy at the gate was the imposter." Davis countered.

"Regardless who he is or what he is up to, he will have to answer some questions about why he was at Aunt Bessie's on the night she was hurt." Charley declared.

*   *   *

Since Jay was involved with some work at the Folsom house, and her dad in Rome with Charley, Amy decided to spend some time with Deidre. She missed the long talks they used to have, and saw this as an opportunity to visit with her one-time roommate and now *stepmother*. Though she dearly loved Deidre, she almost laughed out loud every time someone referred to Deidre as her stepmother. It wasn't just that there were only five years' difference in their ages, but also the reality that they had been as close as sisters before Deidre and her dad had ever thought about matrimony.

"How's married life?" Amy asked when Deidre opened the front door to let her in. "Have you adjusted?"

"I'd say," Deidre responded with a giggle. "So far it has been all a honeymoon, and I have no complaints, but we are talking about your father. You don't want to hear this."

"You're right. Please spare me the details," Amy suggested with a laugh. "The appearance of the place is remarkably better. It just needed a woman's touch."

"It needed that all right. It's been fun, but somewhat of a challenge to transform it from a plain bachelor's quarters to a parsonage for a preacher's family."

They talked about such matters for a few minutes until Amy asked, "Do you have Beau Wilson in any of your classes?"

"Yes, I do. He's in my second period European History class. Why do you ask?"

"Have you noticed he has had a limp recently?" Amy questioned.

"Yes, I did notice that, and I asked him how he injured himself. He told me he sprained his ankle when he jumped off a porch."

"That's what I was afraid of," Amy said. "I thought he might have gotten hurt when he jumped off a porch."

"What do you mean?" Deidre's voice reflected that her friend's statement had her completely baffled. Then the lightbulb came on. "You don't mean... he isn't...."

"That's exactly what I think, but I'm not sure. Let's not tell anyone until we know for sure. We wouldn't want to accuse an innocent boy."

"No, I wouldn't want to do that. I don't think Beau is a bad boy, a little too mischievous perhaps, but not a bad boy," Deidre said as if to convince herself.

They heard a car door slam from the drive and knew that Davis had returned. "Remember, we are to keep this to ourselves until we know for sure, and that means you don't tell your husband," Amy said firmly.

Amy hated to ask Deidre to keep a secret from Davis, but it was important to her that she had all the facts right before preceding any further.

* * *

I hate for anyone to see me like this, Tonya told herself, *but it was good of Charley to come and bring the preacher with him. He's* a great guy, but I was sure he'd totally erased me from his mind long ago.

"Is the younger man that just left the room your significant other?" The nurse approached Tonya's bed with a smile. "He's an attractive guy, and the older gentleman with him isn't bad either."

"No, a lot of girls wish he was their boyfriend, but he's just a friend. The gentleman with him is a preacher," Tonya explained.

"It's not too late, you know. Sometimes romance starts out as friendship," the middle-aged lady dressed totally in white told her. "In fact, that may be the best way. Sometimes it starts with romance and friendship never becomes part of the equation. That can lead to a lot of unhappiness. Lovers also need to be friends. I know all about these matters," the nurse told her. "I've been married three times. I've got a pretty good idea of what works and what doesn't work."

Tonya made a mental note not to seek advice about matters of the heart from this lady as she held her right arm out for the nurse to take her vitals. The left one was in a temporary cast below the elbow as was most of her left leg. *I can't believe I'll be here for several more days and away from work for several weeks. This is a disaster, but maybe it won't be so bad if Charley does return to visit me regularly as he said he would. Since I first met him, I've wanted to get to know him better, but this isn't exactly what I had in mind.* She had taken pain medicine just before Charley and Pastor Morgan came to her room. Her eyes were heavy. She closed them, and in less than three minutes she was out again.

CHAPTER 11

When Davis arrived at the Little Rock Café, four other men were already huddled around the big round table that pretty much had become their exclusive property Monday through Friday mornings. These were all guys who had known each other most of their lives. When Davis returned to his hometown from Indianapolis, he found it enjoyable, despite the constant razzing, to semi-regularly have breakfast with these old high school friends. He had not submitted himself to their sometimes-cruel brand of fellowship since he and Deidre had been married.

"That didn't last long!" Red Edwards owner of the Adairsville Hardware bellowed when he saw Davis approach the table. "Married three weeks, is it? And already you're left to fend for yourself at breakfast."

"Maybe she's not such a good cook, so after she left, he snuck out to find some decent bacon and eggs," Dean Nelson, Charley's brother and the owner of the most successful auto repair shop in town, teased.

Davis seated himself in one of the two empty chairs. "It's been a longtime since any of you guys had breakfast with your wives," he taunted. "I won't even speculate about that state-of-affairs. Deidre had an early engagement at the school, so I thought it might be a good time to take another shot at straightening out you guys. There's never any doubt about where you can be found at this time of the day."

"Preacher, would you see if you can quiet down these trouble-makers? They're a nuisance for the other customers," Brenda, the only waitress the management could persuade to serve this group said with a straight face. "What would you like? I've already taken the orders of these other hard cases at your table."

"Why is it that you are civil to him, but give us such a bad time?" Brad Dwelt, the city fire chief asked the waitress.

"Because he's a gentleman, and you guys are menaces who are set on making my life miserable."

"And you love every second of it," Al Jensen, the local banker suggested.

"Yeah, I love it like I love being bitten by a rattlesnake," Brenda responded.

Davis gave Brenda his order. The waitress turned to head back into the kitchen at which time all four of Davis's companions turned to watch her walk away. She stopped, turned to again face them and hissed, "You guys know I'm a friend of all your wives, and talk with them regularly."

"What? Does she have eyes in the back of her head now?" Brad asked.

"No, she just knows you fellas," Davis spoke up. "You might get a little better service if you show a little more respect."

"She knows we're harmless. It would spoil her day if we didn't give her a hard time," Dean argued.

"Yeah, but there's a limit," Davis scolded. "Maybe you guys need to grow up."

"My, haven't we gotten self-righteous since we've taken a bride?" Brad whined.

"No, he's right," Al agreed. "It's okay to be rude to one another. We know it's all in fun, but we need to treat Brenda more like the lady she is."

"Okay," Dean spoke up after a moment of awkward silence. "I don't know about you guys, but I plan to do better by Brenda, but preacher, don't think that changes my behavior toward you. You already get all the respect you can expect to get."

"I would be disappointed in you if you treated me differently just because I'm a pastor. I expect to receive the same abuse from you that I received when we were in high school."

"Speaking of high school, the football team blew that second playoff game big time, didn't they?" Red commented, obviously to change the subject.

"Yes, but we'll be tough next year, will we not? We lose only a couple of the guys from the offense to graduation, and half the defense will be back," Dean, who had been an outstanding lineman and played both ways in his high school days, said.

"I was sorry to hear about the death of your Aunt Bessie," Al told Dean.

"Yeah, she was a great lady, but ninety-two is a long time to live. I don't expect to last anywhere near that long," the big mechanic replied. "The preacher here will conduct her funeral at the church tomorrow at one o'clock."

Upon her return with their food, Davis could see that Brenda was puzzled by how politely she was treated. After she heard *thank you* and *ma'am* several times, she stopped, looked around the table and asked, "What happened while I was away? Was there a revival or something?"

"Something like that," Al said.

Brenda glanced back several times with a puzzled look on her face as she moved to another table to take orders.

"What do you hear about the Creeper?" Red asked no one in particular.

"I've got my shotgun loaded and ready if he shows up around my house!" Brad declared.

"We don't need any of that kind of talk," Al told his fireman friend. "I haven't heard that he has actually committed any crimes. It's just that he's dressed in a hood with a clown face and shows up in places he shouldn't be at times when he shouldn't be there. I honestly think all the publicity he's gotten in the local paper has encouraged him."

"I hear he paid your daughter a visit the other night," Dean said to Davis.

"Yeah, she wasn't too concerned about it. She picked up a broom and chased him through the neighbor's yard, across the road and through the church parking lot."

"She may be attractive and petite, but you raised a pretty tough gal. I would like to have seen that scene," Al said to Davis with a laugh.

"You're right; she's always taken pretty good care of herself." It wasn't widely known around town that Davis had seen someone in a hoodie near Bessie's house when he found her injured and her dog dead, and Davis kept quiet about that now.

"Well, I've got an engine to pull," Dean told the guys before he got up from the table. His movement motivated the others and they began to disperse.

"Don't forget the tip." The reminder, as always, came from banker, Al Jensen.

Brenda was amazed when she picked up the tips left on the table. *I think I'll pray the preacher will join them more often*, she decided.

* * *

"Another failure! Can't you get the least assignment, right?" The displeasure of the person on the line was clear to the young man with the scar on his right cheek. "You didn't even get inside the fence."

"It wasn't my fault that someone saw me and called the cops. What did you want me to do, stand around and wait for them to arrest me? I've told you, I'll not be locked-up again. You don't know what it's like to be confined to a small cell day after day and night after night."

"Yeah, and the worst of it is you can't get liquor when you're behind bars." The voice nagged. "I want you to try again tonight.

If what we want is in that unit, I don't think we have long to get it out. You'll need a flashlight, but don't use it until you are inside. Wait until well past midnight and park your car behind the building closest to Highway 41. Don't try to go through the gate. Climb over the fence in the back."

"Climb over the fence!" The young man with the scar objected with a loud voice. "There are two strands of barbed-wire across the top of that fence. I'll slice my hands to bits if I do that."

"Don't be such a whiner. Wear heavy gloves. Sometimes I wonder if you have a brain at all. Do what I tell you if you want any more money. They won't let you live at that motel free, you know, and you've got to eat. Again, I'm warning you, stay away from the booze. I know you think you need it, but for once try to get a job done without liquid courage. Don't let me down."

"I'll try." The young man with the scar reluctantly stated.

"Don't try, do it! That's your problem: you have no confidence in yourself. Get it done!" the voice demanded.

The person who made the demands laid the cell phone down. *I probably cut my own throat. I should have hired someone more reliable. I thought I could throw him a bone, but I should've known better.*

*   *   *

Charley agreed to work the Monday night shift so he could attend Aunt Bessie's funeral on Tuesday. Chief Hanson wasn't always big on schedule switches, but he would allow it for a family funeral. Charley stopped by Barton's Funeral home on Summer Street shortly after eight o'clock. The family was there to receive visitors from seven until nine. As much as he would like to, he couldn't spend the evening with the family, but he could drop by, though it would have to be a quick visit and in uniform. "Couldn't you take the night off?" Dean, who stood beside his wife, Sherrie, asked his brother.

"We are shorthanded right now, with several of the guys down with the flu. I agreed to work tonight so I could be off for the funeral tomorrow," Charley explained to him. He strode to the front of the room where Aunt Bessie's body lay in an open coffin. He decided she looked happy and peaceful, and he found comfort in the belief she was indeed as she looked. He shook Pete's hand and hugged Penny. Petey and one of Bessie's other grandsons were in conversation on the other side of the room. He saw them glance his way, and started in their direction when he was intercepted by Davis.

"Are you on duty all night?" Davis inquired.

"Until seven in the morning," Charley responded. "I should be able to get three or four hours of sleep before the funeral. Because I don't want to dishonor Aunt Bessie, I'll try my best not to go to sleep on you tomorrow," he stated with a grin.

Charley was free to patrol any part of the city he wanted, unless he received radio instructions that directed him to a particular place. Since the Creeper had not gotten inside the fence at the storage units on Saturday night, he concluded that if the scary guy was after a specific prize, he might return. He parked in the lot across the road from the gate, turned his lights off, and focused on the storage facility. It was a slow night – not much to be concerned about in the small town on a Monday night. There were no radio messages to call him away from the spot he had chosen, so he stayed put.

It was almost one o'clock and Charley fought to stay awake. He wished he had a cup of coffee. His mind turned to the Lipscomb offer. Sometimes he was sure he would take it, and at other times he was absolutely convinced he didn't want to relocate away from his hometown for any reason. He once heard someone suggest that one of the best ways to make such decisions was to put on paper all the pros and cons. He did that, and the result made it no contest. There were far more reasons to take the offer than to turn it down. Still, he was not convinced.

His mind went to Tonya. He wondered if she was having a good night. When he saw her ten hours earlier, he could see that she was in some pain, but despite her pain, she smiled a lot, and that was good to see. *She's one of a kind*, he decided, *a special lady.* He wondered why he had shied away from her in the two years he had known her. *Any man who lassoes her will get someone special. Maybe that's why I've stayed away over these past months. Maybe I haven't been ready to settle down with someone like her. I think maybe I'm almost there. I don't know if Tonya is the one, but I think I would like to find out. I hope I've not waited too long. A beautiful and personable lady like Tonya may have a dozen guys waiting for her to say yes.*

Suddenly, there was movement that caught Charley's attention on the west side of the storage complex. There was enough illumination from the security lights on the inside of the compound for him to see that someone had made his way over the fence. He saw the figure drop inside and head for the row of bins on the back side of the complex. Charley called for backup, but he felt he did not have time to wait for another officer to arrive. He started his patrol car, drove to the gate, and got out of the car. All the while he kept his eyes posted on the area where the person had disappeared.

Because he had rented a storage bin for himself, Charley knew the code that would open the gate, but he also knew it was not activated to work at this late hour. He would have to climb over the fence. The biggest problem was to get past the two strands of barbed-wire at the top. He felt a little pain when he took hold of the wire to pull him up and he heard cloth rip when he started down the other side. He wore what was almost a new uniform, and now the shirt, no doubt, had a tear in it.

Charley knew it was possible he had, by now, been spotted by the intruder, so he took his gun in hand and cried out. "Police! Come on out now, and we both can avoid any trouble." There was no response. Charley quietly made his way around the corner of the first row of units on the west side and saw no one. He moved on to the next and then the next without as much as a glimpse of anyone or even a sound. Then his heart sank. He heard a loud bang like a gunshot.

CHAPTER 12

C harley ran toward the front gate as fast as he could. He assumed the prowler had looped around the east side to cross the fence at the front gate. When he reached the front, he could see a figure running up the road. Charley put his gun in his holster and swiftly climbed the fence, this time with no regard for hands or uniform. He was ready to open his car door and jump in the driver's seat to chase the villain, who was hightailing it up the road, when he realized what the gun shot he had heard was all about. The tire on the front driver's side was flat. The Creeper, or whoever he was, had shot the tire, and now it was flat. "How could I be so stupid?" Charley asked himself out loud. The Creeper had gotten away again. Before he opened the trunk lid to pull out his spare tire, he looked at the blood that now covered much of the palm of his right hand and then examined the front of his uniform to see several rips on his shirt and trousers. *Wouldn't you know it*; he thought when he looked up to see that his backup had now arrived. *Where was he five minutes ago?* It had already been a long night, and he still had six hours to go. This was one of those moments when he felt very strongly that he should take that job in Savannah.

* * *

With a memorial service to prepare before one o'clock, Davis got to the church office early on Tuesday. A unique lady like Bessie deserved more than a canned funeral message. At nine o' clock Cindy, the church secretary, knocked on his office door and stuck her head in to announce, "Just wanted you to know I'm on the job. Anything I can do for you before I start the regular chores?"

"No," Davis told her. "I plan to prepare for the service this afternoon, so I would appreciate it if you would sort of guard my door unless someone comes in with an emergency."

"I'll do my best," she assured him, "but there are a couple of regulars, and you know who they are, that I couldn't keep away from you with a machine gun."

"You don't need to use any weapons, Cindy. Just encourage them to postpone their visits for a few hours."

It was mid-morning when Davis, decided to take a brief break. He telephoned the 1902 Stock Exchange. "Hello, Janie." He greeted the young clerk when he heard her voice. "You will have to take care of business at the bookshop today since I have a funeral this afternoon."

"I can handle it." she announced. "Mr. Shaw was at the door this morning when I arrived. He wanted to know if you had gotten in any new books by Corra Harris. I told him I didn't know, but showed him where to look for new stock. He didn't find anything."

"It's only been four or five days since he was there. It's impossible to have something new for him every time he shows up when he comes that often," Davis told her.

A little later, Davis finished his tribute to Bessie, and then silently read what he had written. Some of the remarks he intended to make made him a little sad when he read them. He was glad there weren't a lot of those. He wanted to comfort and encourage the family rather than depress them. Davis didn't feel funerals should be gloomy affairs. He also had included in his remarks some humorous memories of their precious Bessie along with some reasons they could be glad for her in her home going. He had confidence that, though less than perfect, his presentation would be a worthy tribute to the lady he so admired, as well as an effective tool to comfort those left behind.

Davis could hear occasional noise from the direction of the kitchen and fellowship hall, and knew the ladies were on the job to prepare what had come to be known as a *funeral dinner*. Davis had always felt this was an extremely effective ministry of the ladies of the congregation. Regardless of whether the deceased was or wasn't a member of their church, they prepared a meal for the family and friends to be served after the committal at the cemetery. Church members had come to expect it and non-members who had enlisted the services of this church's preacher were appropriately impressed by the obvious compassion of the people of the church. It made future ministry to them much more achievable.

Davis was disappointed when time for the service arrived and the three hundred seat auditorium was only half full. *Not a very good turn-out to honor one that was so beloved in our community*, he decided. Then he remembered the words of a funeral director in Indianapolis when he had lamented the sparse attendance for the service of an older gentleman who had been a pillar in their community. "He outlived most of his contemporaries," the undertaker told him. The meager attendance at Bessie's funeral could be explained, in part, by that fact – she had outlived her contemporaries. It was also true that, in modern culture, many people find it much more convenient to stop by the funeral home the night before the funeral rather than attend the funeral itself.

After the service at the church, Davis was surprised that Miss Helen made the effort to be at the graveside committal service. When the small crowd began to disperse, she approached him beside the grave tent with her usual smile. "We've lost another of the old guard," she sadly told him. "There aren't a lot of us left. I enjoyed your service, preacher. It was an honest and optimistic tribute to a fine lady who never accomplished great feats in life, but was such a mighty influence in her own discreet way. I will miss her."

"Thankfully, we still have you around to carry the banner," Davis said with a grin for one of his favorite people. "You can expect me to show up at your door sometime in the next couple weeks, I've got a thirst for a good glass of sweet tea, and I need your help to finish our book."

"What do you mean *our* book? It's **your** book," she declared.

"No, Miss Helen, it's our book. The truth is, it's more your book than mine. Without your columns through the years, there would be no history of Adairsville. I only pulled together material you recorded long ago."

"That's absurd," Miss Helen scolded him. "You just want to make an old lady feel good. You did the work and you need to take the credit."

"Or maybe, the responsibility," Davis remarked. "Let's wait until it's published. Instead of *credit*, the appropriate word may be *blame*," he joked.

* * *

Back at the church fellowship hall, Davis spent time with the family and friends of Bessie Taylor. They traded stories of the colorful lady and enjoyed the delicious food brought in by the church women. When Charley, dressed in suit and tie, came over to speak to him, he noticed his friend had a bandage on his right hand. "What's that about?" he asked, motioning toward the wrapped hand. "I'm sure you couldn't have gotten blisters from hard work."

"I'll tell you about it later. I appreciated your remarks today. I know Aunt Bessie would've approved," Charley offered a rare compliment to Davis.

"I hope she *did*," Davis remarked. "I suspect she heard every word."

Charley understood Davis's point and smiled at the thought. "It's good to have you around when we need you," Charley told his friend as he smiled and walked toward a group of relatives who stood together to jovially trade stories.

It's a shame most families only get together on an occasion such as this, Davis mulled as he observed the small groups gathered around him completely oblivious to others in the room. Many of them, no doubt, were catching up on the lives of their cousins, aunts and uncles and others they had not seen for a while.

"Call the down, out, and up pass. I can beat that safety." The vibrant voice came from behind him, and though Davis had not heard it in almost thirty years, he had no difficulty in putting a name to it. He had often heard that voice when it called plays in a hurdle in his high school days.

He turned to face the person who approached him with a wide smile, Davis cheerfully announced, "I don't believe it. It's the old quarterback himself. How has life treated you, Bobby Thornton? Have you thrown any touchdown passes lately?" he asked.

"How could I? I don't have my number one receiver," the handsome man, an inch taller and a few pounds lighter than Davis declared as he extended a hand to Davis, to eagerly greet him. "How many touchdown passes did we hook up for in our senior year?"

"I think it was seven," Davis told him.

"You *think*? You *know* exactly how many, and you could tell me the details of every one of them," The one-time high school quarterback declared.

"Where've you been?" Davis asked. "I lost track of you."

"I've lived in Carrollton for the last six years. I opened a real estate business there after I spent several years in a classroom while I tried coaching football in the West Georgia Region," Bobby told him. "I was surprised to find you back in the old hometown. I thought you had gone on to bigger and better endeavors."

"After college and seminary, we lived in Richmond, Virginia for a time before I went to Indianapolis. After Julie's death, it felt right to return home."

"I'd heard Julie passed away, I'm sure sorry about that, pal. She was a great gal. You two were made for one another," Davis's high school friend told him.

"She was the other half of *me*," Davis said and dropped his head. "I sometimes wondered if I would be able to go on, but the Lord has fixed that. He gave me a wonderful girl who is very much like Julie in some ways, and very different in others. We were married less than a month ago, and life is special again."

"That's wonderful! Is she here? I would love to meet her," Bobby stated. He turned his head to look at the people around him. No doubt, he thought he could pick out Mrs. Davis Morgan.

"No, she couldn't make it. She's a teacher and since she took a week off for our honeymoon, she felt she shouldn't be out of the classroom today," Davis told him. "I'm surprised to see you here; did you know Bessie well?"

"Yes, I can't remember when I didn't know her. She was a neighbor of ours when I was in elementary school. In fact, she used to babysit me and my sister on occasion. I've loved and admired her for a long time."

"I understand several members of her family also live in Carrollton. Have you maintained contact with them?" Davis inquired.

"Yes, her son and daughter Pete and Penny live in the area, but I seldom see any of them. I did have Penny as a real estate client two or three years back, but that has been about the extent of it," Bobby explained.

"What about P.W.? I understand he also resides down that way?" Davis asked.

"You mean Pete's son, Petey? Don't get me started on him. He's well known around town as a boozehound. I think he spends most of his time in bars to impress the ladies with stories about all the important people his grandmother knew. Petey isn't one of my favorite people."

Davis filed that information away in his mind. Perhaps it would be useful later. The two men spent a few more minutes together to catch up and talk about their glory days of high school athletics. Davis loved the opportunity to spend time with his long lost old friend, and decided that a class reunion would be a fun event. He would have to see if he could find an old classmate or two to spearhead such an occasion.

Before he left the church, Charley approached Davis. "Sometime over the next few days, when you have a little time, I need to get together with you about the stuff Aunt Bessie wanted you to have out of that storage unit. If we can clear it out before the end of the month, the estate won't have to pay rent for January. Let me know when you are available. There may be enough stuff to require a pick-up to haul it all away unless you want to make several loads with that Jeep."

"I'll see if I can borrow a pick-up from one of the guys in the church," Davis told him. Davis looked around to make sure no one could hear before he asked. "Where are you at with that decision? Have you come to any conclusions yet?"

"No, I think I'll give myself another week. It seems one day I'm sure of one direction and the next day, the other."

"Please know I continue to pray about it every day," Davis told him.

"I know that, and I appreciate it. I'm glad I have another person with whom I can talk about it," Charley told him with a half-smile.

CHAPTER 13

Rather than go home immediately after the funeral dinner, Davis drove to Floyd Medical Center in Rome to visit with two elderly church members who were patients there. He found Grace Padget, who had fallen and broken her right hip, to be much improved since his last visit. Davis was amazed at her attitude. Grace, a widow, lived with her younger sister, and was many years past the time when she initially became a recipient of Social Security. "Grace, you look fantastic, how are you feeling?" Davis asked her.

"I feel like a million dollars, preacher. I'll be back in church in no time."

A few minutes later when Davis got to Gene Barnes's room, he found a man with a totally different outlook. Though Gene was a few years younger and had an injury much less serious than Grace's, he went on and on about how poorly life had treated him. It always dumbfounded Davis to observe such opposite mindsets from two people in much the same circumstances. What causes some people to see, almost exclusively, the dark side of life, while others are drawn to the light? Davis's mind went to a passage of scripture that had long ago become one of his favorites, *"Finally, brothers, whatever is true, whatever is noble, whatever is right, whatever is pure, whatever is lovely, whatever is admirable – if anything is excellent or praiseworthy – think about such things."* (Philippians 4:8).

Davis decided that would be his subject on Sunday: "*We Are What We Think.*"

Though Tonya Willis wasn't part of his congregation, he stopped by her room for a brief visit.

"Hi, Tonya, I'm Davis Morgan. You may not remember me from my visit with you a couple of days ago. You were heavily sedated when Charley and I came in."

"Sure, I remember you, preacher. You're the guy with the pretty wife who was with Bessie Taylor when we were called to her house."

"That's me, the guy with the pretty wife. That's my claim to fame," Davis responded with a laugh. "That and the fact I am a friend of Charley Nelson's."

"There are worse circumstances than to have Charley for a friend. He has been here every day since I was admitted," Tonya told Davis. "Not even my own brothers have made it that often, nor would I expect them to."

"I seem to remember that Solomon wrote in Proverbs "... *there is a friend who sticks closer than a brother*" (Proverbs 18:24). Charley has been that kind of friend to me. He has been there for me every time I've needed him over the past year. I don't have a brother, but I can't imagine that anyone could be more loyal than Charley has been. I think the guy is terrific," Davis informed her. "But I'm not here to sing Charley's praises. I suspect he would be significantly embarrassed by such testimony on his behalf. Are you on the mend?" Davis asked her.

"I'm well, under the circumstances. I have two breaks in my left leg and one in my lower left arm, but the doctor says I should heal back to normal in time. They don't seem to be overly concerned by the concussion at this point. I learned just a few minutes ago that I will probably be dismissed tomorrow or the day after. I won't be able to put weight on the leg for a while, so I must hobble around on crutches and one leg for a time. Even with the lower location, the break in my arm makes that much more difficult. I guess I won't be allowed back to work for three months or so. It's shaping up to be an enormously boring recuperation," Tonya added with a look of sadness that clouded her features. "I never learned any kind of needlework, and I usually find TV to be mind-numbing."

"Do you enjoy reading?" Davis asked her. "It might be the time to pull out a good book or two."

"I like physical activity, but since that won't be feasible, to read sounds like the best alternative," The young woman replied.

"Tell me what kind of books you like, and I'll enlist Charley to deliver you a stack of them," Davis offered.

"I guess I like mysteries about as well as any category," she told him.

"What about Agatha Christie? I have a giant collection of those," Davis announced. "If you're interested, I will send you several. When you get tired of those, we'll find some other variation."

"Sounds great," Tonya told him and forced a smile. "It's kind of you to do that for me."

They talked a while longer before Davis concluded their visit with a prayer. On his way out of her room, he wondered about Tonya's spiritual status.

* * *

Amy was at a table in a conference room next to the administrative offices at Adairsville High School. Jim Ralston, an assistant principal was also in the room when Beau Wilson, who had been summoned by intercom, entered.

"Sit down, Beau," Amy motioned toward an empty chair across the table from where she was positioned. "Do you know why I called you here today?"

Beau's face paled before he spoke. "No Ma'am, I don't have any idea," he stuttered in an unconvincing tone.

"Why were you limping recently?" She asked the seventeen-year-old senior whose legs slightly bounced and his fingers lightly tapped the table top.

After a moment of silence, he answered, "I sprained my ankle."

"Did you sprain it when you jumped off my porch?" Amy asked.

"No ma'am, I've never been on your porch, Mrs. Archer. I'm not sure I know exactly where you live." Beau sounded a little defensive.

"Do you own a black hoodie?"

"I have several hoodies. I don't believe I have a black one," he stated.

"Beau, I know it was you who was recently on my porch in a black hoodie and clown make-up. I saw your face clearly when our eyes met through the window. At the time, I couldn't put a name to the face, but I knew it was familiar. By the next day, I figured it out, and when you came to school with a limp, I knew I was right. There is no reason for you to lie. You're not a convincing liar, and I guess that's good."

Beau sat for a few moments while he examined his feet, obviously not sure what to say next. He raised his head, but avoided the gaze of the teacher across the table, finally he said. "It all started as a joke. Linda Peace constantly tormented us, and we thought it would be funny to scare her. I put on clown make-up and hoodie. Actually, my hoodie isn't black. It's navy blue. I stationed myself outside her bedroom window, and when she walked-in, I made enough noise to make sure she saw me. When that happened, she turned around, ran back the way she entered and screamed as if she were being murdered. I just scared her. It wasn't like I was a peeping Tom or a pervert. Then it just kind-of took off, and we decided it was our obligation to keep the myth alive. I didn't even know whose house I was at when I showed up on your front porch. I was as surprised to see you as you were to see me."

"Do you have any idea how much worry you've caused the people of this town?" Amy asked. "You are lucky you weren't shot. I know people who have bought guns for protection against the Adairsville Creeper," she informed him. "There are a few nuts who can't wait to get a shot at you."

"We didn't give it much thought. Part of the fun was that we could make a clean get-away after we were spotted."

"I would strongly recommend from this time on, you make a point to think before you act. It might prove to be crucial to you and the people around you in your future life," Amy scolded. "Several times you've used the pronoun, we. Am I correct in presuming, there was someone else involved along with you in this stunt?

A minute or two passed before Beau answered. "I don't want to get someone else in trouble by being a tattle, but it's true. There were two Creepers. Sometimes I wore the clown make-up, and at other times it was him. The Creeper never acted alone. Whichever was not in make-up was always in the shadows somewhere nearby. Please don't make me tell you who he is."

"I won't make you do that, but please know, it won't be hard to identify your partner now that we know you were involved. Both of you need to come clean before this day ends," Amy sternly stated.

"I've a couple more questions. Why were you out near Pine Log at Mrs. Taylor's house on the Saturday night she was injured?"

"I don't know Mrs. Taylor or where she lives, and I haven't been anywhere near Pine Log in months," Beau answered forcefully. "I promise you, we never hurt anyone."

"I believe you," Amy responded. "What about the storage bins behind the hardware store? Did you or your partner try to break-in there?"

"No, we didn't. All we did was scare some people. We never stole anything. We didn't break-in anywhere," Beau assured her. "We always did the Creeper stunt in town within a short distance of the depot."

"I will trust that you've told me the truth. Here is what I want you to do," she instructed. "Talk with your partner in this little scheme. Tell him you've been found-out, and the best plan now is for you to confess. The two of you then need to go to the police station, and ask for Chief Hanson or Charley Nelson. Tell whichever you talk with what you've told me today. I don't know the laws in these matters. You have managed to scare the living daylights out of some people and get an entire town riled-up, but I'm almost certain the only criminal act of which you have been legally guilty is to trespass. I think that can be worked out if you will confess. That needs to be taken care of before it goes any further and you find yourself in a lot of trouble or worse."

"I'll talk with him. I can't speak for him, but I promise you I'll go to the police today," he told her.

"You need to make your cohort see that it will be best for him to do the same. It could very well mean jail time for him if he doesn't," Amy warned. "Now you go and do what's right, and don't you ever pull a stunt like this again."

Beau got up and walked toward the door, then stopped and turned to again face his English teacher, "Mrs. Archer, thank you for not tattling and for allowing me to take care of this myself. There's one other fact I want to tell you. I had no idea you could run so fast," he said with a smile on his face. "I thought for sure you would catch me with that broom and beat me half to death."

CHAPTER 14

"**D**id you hear?" Janie asked Davis who was busy dusting bookshelves on Wednesday morning. "They caught the Adairsville Creeper. I heard he walked into the police chief's office and gave himself up."

"No, I haven't heard that news" Davis told the clerk immediately while he turned his attention to her.

"You're slipping. I can't believe I got wind of some news before you. I would have thought your friend Charley would've spilled his guts by now," Janie stated with a smug tone to her voice.

"When did this happen?" Davis asked.

"My source said it was late yesterday," Janie responded. "Maybe four-thirty or five o'clock."

"Charley was off duty for his Aunt's funeral yesterday, and besides he doesn't tell me everything. There are certain matters he, as a police officer, must keep confidential," Davis reminded her.

"Yeah, that's your story. Everybody knows he spills his guts to you."

"*Everybody*, it seems, think they know a lot more than they really do. I would be careful not to put much stock in what you hear from *everybody*." Davis told Janie, but felt a little like a hypocrite since he knew there were few matters in which Charley withheld information from him. "Tell me Janie, did your source tell you the identity of the Creeper?"

"I haven't heard a name, only that it was a high school student," Janie informed him.

If Janie knew more, evidently, she had decided to keep it from him. She turned and went back to the front where she stationed herself behind the checkout counter. Davis continued to do busy work in the shop. He stopped occasionally to help a potential customer. A couple of those patrons mentioned the news about the Creeper, but they had no more details than those Janie had given him.

Around noon, Davis announced to Janie, "I think I'll walk down the street to the Inn for lunch. Call me if you need me."

"With perhaps a stop at the police station?" Janie, who knew him well asked with a smile. "You can't wait to get the details, can you?"

Davis did not verbally respond to her remark, but gave her a dirty look before he smiled and went through the door.

An officer in uniform sat behind the reception desk when Davis entered the home of the Adairsville police force. "Hello chaplain, can I help you?" the officer asked.

"I would like to speak with Charley for a moment if he is around," Davis responded.

"Charley's on patrol." the veteran police officer told him. "If it's important, I can contact him and have him call you."

"No, don't do that. It's not that important. If he happens to come in anytime today, ask him to either call me or stop by my shop when he has time,"

"Incidentally, tell your daughter that she did a good job," The officer at the desk said to Davis as he was about to leave.

"My daughter? What do you mean?" Davis asked with a bewildered look.

"You know ... with the Creeper situation!"

The statement baffled Davis, but then he remembered how Amy had chased the Creeper with the broom.

"I'll tell her," He said while he formed a mental picture of Amy with broom in hand behind a hooded figure that ran across the yard.

The first person Davis saw when he entered the Inn was Sam Ellison, the flamboyant mayor who Davis had avoided for days.

The mayor wanted the history of Adairsville finished yesterday, but Davis, with his new duties as interim pastor, had not found time to add the final touches. He knew he could expect a reprimand from the mayor who took his duties very seriously. "Come over here and sit with us," the mayor called out with what sounded more like a command than an invitation.

"No, I appreciate your invitation, but I don't want to interrupt your lunch," Davis told him when he walked over to stand beside the table where the mayor and a man Davis did not know were seated.

"Nonsense," the mayor insisted. "There's an important matter I need to talk with you about. This gentleman is Ross Douglas, a salesman with which the city does business. We're just about through with our meal, but we can visit for a couple of minutes."

"I'm Davis Morgan," Davis extended his hand to the other gentleman at the table. "I'm pleased to meet you Mr. Douglas. So, you don't live in our fair town," Davis surmised.

"No, I live in Dalton, but Sam has done his best to convince me to relocate."

"You might do well to listen to him. Dalton has a lot going for it, but there's no place like Adairsville. You'll not find better people anywhere than you'll find right here in this little town."

"Pretty Boy Floyd grew up right over there across the railroad tracks," Sam excitedly remarked and pointed to the south.

"That's not exactly the kind of people I had in mind," Davis reacted. "But that's true. As a boy, he lived in the little gray house behind the depot."

"Speaking of bad guys, I was sure impressed with your gal, Amy, single-handedly bringing the Creeper to his knees. Chief Hanson gave me a full report earlier. She's a chip off the old block," the mayor said loud enough for just about everyone in the restaurant to hear.

Davis wondered why now, several days after the incident, everyone was so excited about Amy's encounter with the Creeper.

After the waitress took his order, Sam looked straight at him with a doubtful stare before he asked, "Well, how's our book progressing? Is it ready for publication?" Then there was silence as he waited for an answer.

I knew it wouldn't take him long to get to that subject. "I promise you, Sam, I'll have it ready in two or three weeks. Give me a little more time. We want the finished product to be a book of which the people of our town can be proud. I've taken on a lot of responsibility lately, and that has slowed me down a bit. Just a little more time and it will be in the hands of the publisher."

"Well, we've waited this long, I suppose we can wait a couple more weeks," the impatient mayor conceded. "But I will hold you to that, two more weeks."

"I said two *or three weeks*, and I will have it ready by then, even if I have to go without sleep some nights." Davis assured him.

Sam and his salesman friend excused themselves before Davis was served. It didn't take him long to devour the light lunch he had ordered, and then he was on his way back to the shop.

* * *

About the middle of the afternoon, Charley appeared at the Corra Harris Bookshop. "I hear you need to talk with me," Charley bellowed out to Davis from across the room.

"Yes, I understand the Adairsville Creeper gave himself up. I'm an interested party, you know. Do you have any news for me?" Davis asked.

"I figured you already had the details since it was your daughter who orchestrated it," Charley's face showed surprise as he spoke.

"My daughter?" Davis raised his voice, obviously flabbergasted by the news. "What did she have to do with it?"

"Didn't she tell you? Amy recognized the boy in the costume who showed up on her back porch. She confronted him and talked him into giving himself up. There were actually two of them who came in. Evidently it was just a teenage prank."

"What about Bessie? That was no prank." Davis emphatically responded.

"The boys claim they had no part in that, nor the break-in at the storage facility." Charley told him. "The chief believes they are telling the truth, but who knows? They may have pulled the wool over our eyes." Charley speculated.

"Then if their story holds up, that means we have a copycat, or perhaps two, in our midst," Davis concluded.

"That would seem to be the case. The Creeper demanded a lot of attention. Whoever injured Aunt Bessie to rummage through her house and later broke into the storage center, perhaps thought he could divert attention away from himself, and put the blame on the scary guy in the black hoodie," Charley surmised. "You and your daughter need to communicate more," Charley suggested.

"That's what happens when they grow up and get married. They don't talk to you anymore," Davis said with a brief laugh, but in reality, there was an element of seriousness to his words. He didn't like that he was no longer his daughter's number one confidant.

"You'll be glad to know that I have a date with your tenant tonight. Randi and I plan to go out to dinner," Charley announced.

"Seems like you two are getting along rather well, and to be honest, that surprises me. She made it clear to some of us early on that she wouldn't be interested in a small-town policeman," Davis said.

"But that was before she knew me. How can any girl not be attracted to this face and this personality?" Charley jested while he pointed toward himself.

"Maybe so, but I don't see it," his friend teased.

"That's because you're not a beautiful, young and eligible female. They can't help themselves. They love me even when they try not to."

"I think it's time you got back out on patrol. It's gotten a little deep in here," Davis joshed. On his way out, Charley stopped to see if he could make Janie smile. Davis picked up his cell phone to call Amy. He knew her last class had concluded about ten minutes earlier, and he certainly had a concern he needed to discuss with her.

* * *

"Tell me about life in the big city of Nashville," Charley suggested to Randi as they waited for their orders to be served. Charley preferred the Adairsville Inn or another restaurant that specialized in good ole American or Southern cuisine, but Randi chose El Nopal.

"Oh, I guess it was much like any city in the South. We were a relatively typical family. Dad built up a moderately successful business, a hardware store, which he eventually sold to a large chain, but continued to manage until he retired," Randi told him.

"Do you have brothers and sisters?" Charley asked.

"I have two brothers, one older than me who is a career military man. He's a captain in the army stationed in Florida right now. He has a wife and two lovely children," she informed her escort.

"And what about your other brother, where is he and what does he do?" Charley asked.

"Who knows?" Randi said with a frown on her face. "Andy's my twin brother. He's the black sheep of the family, and kind of hard to keep up with. I'd just as soon not talk about him."

They continued to chat while they munched on tortilla chips until Charley heard a voice from behind him. "It looks like you're making out all right, cousin."

Charley turned to see Petey with a young woman he did not recognize. "Hello Petey, I thought you would be back in Carrollton by now." Charley had a look of disappointment on his face.

"I'll stay around here until Grandma's estate is settled, and I get what's rightfully mine," he informed them.

"Randi, this is my cousin, Petey, I mean P.W. Taylor. P.W., this is Randi Metcalf, our girls' basketball coach."

Randi looked away from Petey as she shyly said, "Pleased to meet you."

Petey continued to stare at Charley's attractive date before finally his mouth flew open, and he declared, "I know you. You once lived in Carrollton."

"No, I never lived in Carrollton. I lived in Bremen before I moved here," she told him.

"That's just a few miles up the road from Carrollton. I remember you," P.W. insisted.

"I'm sure we've never met," Randi remarked with a red face.

"If you say so, but I would never forget a beautiful face like yours," P.W. said with a half-smile before he took the hand of his companion to march across the room toward their assigned table while he glanced back toward them every five seconds or so.

"Sorry about that," Charley apologized to his date. "You spoke a moment earlier of black sheep. That's ours."

"I understand," Randi said. She was pleasant all evening, but Charley noticed she was quieter than usual.

CHAPTER 15

"What a beautiful day," Davis remarked to Janie while he stood at the front door of the 1902 Stock Exchange and gazed out at the sunshine. It was one of those winter days which north Georgia occasionally provides much to the delight of its citizens. It was late morning and the sky was a deep blue with no clouds in sight. The temperature was already above sixty, and per the forecast Davis heard earlier, it would exceed seventy by midafternoon.

"And I'm trapped inside this establishment until five o'clock this afternoon," Janie lamented.

"Not me," Davis's face lit up as he spoke. "After lunch, I think I'll play a little baseball."

"You better be careful. You're not as young as you once were. You don't want to pull or damage some part you haven't used for a while." Janie chuckled. She obviously liked to rag Davis about his age.

"I'll have you to know I can still outdistance some men half my age," he snapped. He knew his claim was a half-truth at best.

"Maybe if they're on crutches or in a wheelchair," the playful young clerk countered.

Davis went back to his shop and took his cell phone from his pocket. "Hello Charley. I've given it some thought, and I think I've come up with an idea about how we can catch the guy in the black hoodie who injured Bessie and attempted to break into the storage facility...."

Charley interrupted Davis, "He didn't just injure Aunt Bessie, he killed her. The cause of death officially might be natural causes, but it was that blow to the head that eventually ended her life."

"I suspect you're right, and that's one of the reasons I would like to see him caught and behind bars as soon as possible. I think you would agree that it's reasonable to assume it was the same guy who broke into the storage space that did the damage at Bessie's place. I saw someone in a black hoodie leave Bessie's place the evening the damage was done. Twice someone in a black hoodie was spotted when he tried to get into the storage facility where Bessie's valuables are stored. It makes sense that someone is after an item or items that belonged to her."

"That makes sense to me, but I can't ascertain that there are any real valuables that he could be after. As Bessie's executor, I have gone through her house as well as the storage bin, and found nothing that could incite such behavior," Charley declared.

"It may not be among her possessions, but rather what the culprit *thinks* is there," Davis suggested. "Here's my idea. Obviously, he hasn't yet gotten into the storage unit. Why don't we casually get word out by every means possible that you'll empty the bin on Saturday afternoon? At that time, you'll distribute what is there to the people Bessie designated. Today is Thursday, so we would have a couple of days to discreetly stake it out, and wait for the potential burglar to make his move. My guess is he'll want to get to whatever he is after before the stuff is dispersed among several people."

There was a moment of silence after which Charley stated, "That sounds like a feasible plan. I will run it by the chief to see what he thinks about the stake-out. You know how the chief feels about such issues. He'll not want you anywhere near that unit over the next two or three days while the sting is in progress."

"That's not a problem," Davis replied. "I've promised Deidre I will stay away from those kinds of situations. You guys on the force can handle it without any interference from me."

"Is this really Davis Morgan to whom I'm speaking, the same one who instigated the trap that resulted in the capture of the Rat-Faced Man, and the one who brought to justice the mad man with the bow and arrow? No, I'm sure it's an imposter. This couldn't be Davis Morgan."

"It's me all right. It's the new Davis Morgan, the one who doesn't meddle in police affairs," Davis assured him in the most convincing tone he could muster.

"I believe that like I believe winter is now over in North Georgia. It can't happen!" Charley emphatically announced. "It's not possible! Spread the word about Saturday." Charley quickly changed the course of conversation before he hung up.

Davis, as usual, was left a tad annoyed by Charley's haste to get off the phone. He proceeded to call George Black. "George, would you take care of a chore for me?"

"Sure, I will preacher, if it's possible."

"If he's not busy, would you ask Tommy to meet me out at Manning Mill Park at two o'clock this afternoon, and bring his ball glove with him?"

"He's not here right now, but I doubt he's doing anything important unless he's at work on those bookshelves out at Mr. Shaw's place today. I'll give him a ring and pass on your message."

"I would appreciate it. Give me a call when you learn if he's available. This weather is too perfect to stay inside all day. It's the kind of day made to throw the baseball around," Davis concluded.

"Tommy would like that, preacher. He would like that a lot, and I appreciate that you thought of him," George responded.

"Maybe he'll be able to give me some pointers, though there are those who believe it's too late," Davis said when he looked toward the front where Janie stood behind the checkout counter.

* * *

Davis arrived at Manning Mill Park ten minutes before two. Tommy was already there. He was seated on one of the bleachers with his mitt on his left hand and a baseball in his right. He stood up when he saw Davis, who wore a baseball cap and a sweatshirt, get out of his Jeep and stroll toward the diamond with glove, bat and ball in hand.

Baseball had for many years held a special place in the hearts of a lot of people in this section of Georgia. The industrial leagues, sponsored by the large factories in the area, were a fixture from the early twentieth-century until the middle nineteen-fifties. It was a welcome diversion for the hard-working people who labored in those mills and often lived in the little mill villages. Hundreds of people would gather at the various stadiums for weekend games that were taken quite seriously. It was said, by the old-timers, that the quality of play in those leagues was as good as in many of the professional farm teams of that era.

Tommy's grandfather, Thomas Black, for whom Tommy was named, had been a star shortstop in the North Georgia Industrial League. He had even gone on to play some major-league baseball in the midst of the talent thin World War II years. Tommy was proud of his baseball heritage and had longed to follow in the footsteps of his namesake. His knee injury and the surgery that followed a couple of years back had brought an abrupt halt to his rapid and impressive rise in the sport.

"Thanks for meeting me," Davis greeted the eager young man who was already on his way to the infield area. "I need to get the old right arm limbered up with some short tosses for a few minutes." Davis had been a decent high school catcher, and had excelled in summer baseball which he played in nearby Calhoun; however, it had been a long time. The body was not as strong or as limber as it once had been. Throwing the ball while only forty or fifty feet apart gave Davis an opportunity to both get limber and to talk with Tommy. They talked baseball for a few minutes. Then, when Tommy opened the door for him to approach other matters, he didn't hesitate. He understood that he might not have future opportunities.

"Tommy, you know your dad has been awfully worried about you. He's concerned about the direction your life has taken."

"I'm a little troubled about that myself," Tommy responded. "It seems like there is nothing left for me. It's just, get up each day and endure more of the same. That's not what I expected adult life to be like."

"That's not the way it has to be," Davis told him. "Life can be fun. It can provide us with fulfillment and even excitement when we live it the way God intended for it to be lived," Davis jumped to catch a ball thrown slightly above his head.

"That's easy for you to say, you have a lot of stuff to live for. You've gotten opportunities. All the doors have closed for me," Tommy whined.

"I know circumstances have thrown you a curve, Tommy. Your dreams haven't materialized, but that often happens. You are not an exception. We must learn to move on, to find new dreams and new goals for our lives. Make your own opportunities. I'll tell you this, not much ever came from sitting around feeling sorry for yourself, or attempting to drown your troubles. I have a higher opinion of you than that, Tommy. It's true what they say, life to a large degree is what we make it. Don't let circumstances control the success or failure of your life. I've had to learn that myself in recent years. I will terminate my sermon now and concentrate on why we are here, but I want you to promise me you'll give serious consideration to what I've said."

"You've given me something to chew on, Preacher. I promise you I'll think about it," Tommy meekly replied.

"And will you do one more thing for me? Don't call me preacher out here on the ball field. My name is *Davis*. I think I'm limber now. Do you want to take a few ground balls?" Tommy went to the shortstop position. Davis at home plate took his wooden thirty-three-inch bat that had served him well through the years, and started to hit ground balls to the young man in the space between second and third base. At first Davis held back, careful not to hit the ball hard, but after a few minutes he swung the bat hard and Tommy gloved every ball that came anywhere near him. Davis watched Tommy move and couldn't believe this boy had major knee surgery two years earlier.

"If it's okay with you, I would like to hit a few," Tommy requested.

"We can do that, but I only brought a couple of balls."

"I have a full bag," Tommy replied while he trotted over to where he had been seated when Davis arrived. He brought the bag to Davis on the mound and dumped them at his feet before he headed to the plate to pick up the bat. Davis lobbed the first pitch across the plate and Tommy connected to hit the ball a good forty feet over the left field fence. With each delivery, Davis put a little more heat on the pitch, but still Tommy cleared the fence one out of every three times. *This kid has what it takes to make it*, he decided.

When there were no more balls left to pitch, Davis and Tommy walked together to the outfield to gather them. While they walked side by side Davis asked Tommy, "What can you tell me about this Bertram Shaw for whom you work? What kind of guy is he?"

"He's been good to me, but he's not a man with a lot of patience. What he wants, he wants right now. He's been fair with me, probably paid me more than I deserve since I don't know much about carpentry. I really don't have any complaints about him." Tommy added.

"I'm glad to hear that. I've talked with him briefly a couple of times. I really haven't gotten to know him well, but since we have a mutual interest in collectable books, that will probably change," Davis suggested. "If you see him in the next couple of days, tell him Charley will let me get the stuff out of Bessie Taylor's storage Saturday afternoon. That could mean I will soon have some

Corra Harris memorabilia. I know he has shown real interest in such collectables."

"I'm scheduled to work at his place tomorrow, so I'll be sure to tell him," Tommy declared.

For the next fifteen minutes Tommy pitched to Davis who hit only two over the fence, but did connect for a few solid line drives.

"Let's sit down over here on the bench for a few minutes," Davis suggested after they had again bagged all the balls. "It looks to me like that knee has healed rather well. Does it give you any trouble?"

"Not really. I still run well, but I don't have the quickness I once had. I'm probably a second or third baseman rather than a shortstop now," Tommy explained.

"I have a friend who was in my church in Indianapolis who played some pro ball. He's still a part-time scout for the Boston Red Sox. I'll give him a call tonight and tell him about the potential I see in you. You may never hear from him, or you might get a call from him in the next few days. Spring training is just around the corner. If I were you, I would start to work myself into the best physical shape possible, as well as get my life back together. Now remember, there are no guarantees. But if this doesn't pan out, there'll be other opportunities, perhaps in baseball or in some other field," Davis assured him.

Tommy was beside Davis on the bench with his mouth wide open and a stunned look on his face. "You mean there's a chance...," he finally blurted out.

"It may be a longshot, but there's a chance." Davis assured him.

"That's all I ask for, just a longshot – a chance!" The excited young man exclaimed.

Have I done the young man a disservice by planting this hope? Davis wondered. *If so, he will totally fall apart if it doesn't work out, but from what I've seen today, I believe he can make it if he'll allow the Lord to pull his life back together.*

CHAPTER 16

Davis called Deidre who had only moments earlier gotten home from a long day of school. "Charley told me his friend Tonya is quite depressed at home alone and needs some company," he informed her. "I know you must be tired, but I wondered if after dinner you could go with me to see if maybe we can bring a little sunshine to her day. I figured that could be accomplished more easily if you were along. To save time and give you a little room to breathe, I'll go by Zaxby's and get some chicken for dinner."

"I would like to visit with Tonya, and the chicken idea sounds wonderful. Seems like a good plan for a Thursday night," Deidre replied.

After dinner, Davis took a quick shower and dressed. Afterwards he telephoned to get permission to visit Tonya and they were on their way. They drove just over ten minutes south on interstate 75 to reach her home near the little community of White. On the way, Davis told Deidre about his afternoon at the park with Tommy.

"Yeah, it's hard work, but somebody must do it," she teased, when he told her about the time they spent on the baseball diamond.

"Don't let me forget to call my friend Tim in Indianapolis when we get back home. I think the call will benefit both him and Tommy."

Davis followed the directions Tonya gave him over the phone, and they pulled into the driveway of a neat little bungalow. The small, light-covered cedar tree which grew by the porch which Tonya had described confirmed they were at the correct house.

After she opened the door and let them in, Tonya hobbled back to her chair and invited them to sit on the sofa. It struck Davis how difficult it must be for Tonya to get around even on crutches with broken left arm and leg. *It would be impossible if the break on the arm had been above the elbow,* he thought, *and for the average person, impossible even with the current situation. She is, no doubt, a strong motivated girl.*

"Thank you for your thoughtfulness. I talked with Charley on the phone, but I haven't seen another soul all day long. It's good to see other human faces. I'm a little concerned that I recently started to talk to myself," Tonya told them.

"I guess it's because Charley respects you so much that I've looked forward to getting to know you. He can't stop talking about what a special person you are," Deidre revealed to the girl who looked a little surprised.

"I didn't know how good a friend Charley is until this happened. He's been super supportive throughout the whole ordeal. Incidentally, I do appreciate the books you had Charley deliver to me. I've read about half of them already." Tonya announced.

"I suspect you've gotten tired of Miss Marple and Hercule Poirot by now." Davis said with a chuckle.

"Oh no, we've become best of friends. It's been fun getting acquainted with them."

"If not before, I will see Charley on Saturday when we clean out his Aunt Bessie's storage unit. I'll find more books for him to deliver to you," Davis promised.

"I certainly was sorry to hear of Mrs. Taylor's death. I didn't know her, but had heard neat stories about her for years. And, of course, when we attend to someone, I guess I feel a kinship to them, and it's always hard when we find out that they don't make it."

Their visit with the injured young woman was pleasant, and when they left after about forty-five minutes, they felt as if they had known Tonya for a long time. "I plan to come hear you preach when I'm able to get out of this house," she said when they got up to leave.

"You come and we'll sit together. My husband is usually too busy to sit with me for Sunday services," Deidre told her with a straight face and then grinned.

"She's my top pick for Charlie," Deidre told Davis on their way home. "I like her a lot."

"What about Randi? Weren't you gung-ho to get the two of them together earlier?" Davis asked.

"Randi is all right, but I can see a lot of friction in their relationship, should they become a couple. It seems to me that their separate goals and interests would create conflict. They'll probably get along well as long as it is simply a social situation, but I don't see them in a serious relationship," Deidre suggested.

"We'll see, I'm sure you know a lot more about the grounds for compatibility in such relationships than I do, but it surely appears Charley and Randi are getting along great. In fact, he was to have dinner with her tonight," Davis informed her.

* * *

Charley met Randi at the Adairsville Inn after she had allowed her young athletes to go home from practice a little earlier than normal. "It's unusual for us not to have a Thursday night game, but this week we play both Friday and Saturday. The girls have worked hard, and I thought they deserved the break," she told Charley.

"Do you like being a basketball coach? Is that what you plan to do with the rest of your life?" Charley inquired.

"It's okay. I've always loved sports. It was a big part of my experience in both high school and college, but I don't know that I want to teach and coach for the rest of my life. I guess that since I'm now all grown up, I should start to think beyond my childhood obsession, but I've not decided what direction I'll take, and for now coaching suits me fine."

"I do agree with one of your statements, you are definitely all grown up," Charley stared at his dinner companion with an appreciative smile.

"What about you, Charley? Do you plan to be a policeman for the rest of your life?" Randi asked.

"That's the way I planned it. My father was once the chief here in Adairsville. I guess that sounds more impressive than it should. When he started, he was the chief and the entire force. He protected the city all by himself for several years. He even patrolled in his own car. He was my hero, and all I ever wanted was to be like him. I worked in Dean's garage for a couple of years after high school until I spent some time at the police academy and the powers that be decided I was ready for a spot in the department. Dean has constantly pressured me to be his partner at the garage, but that has never been a temptation for me. I hope you won't tell anyone...." Charley looked around as he spoke. "But recently I've received an offer that does interest me a lot. I enjoy flying a great deal. For me, it's about the only activity that can compete with law enforcement." Charley took a sip of water before he continued.

"A very wealthy business man has offered me a lot of money and great benefits to be his private pilot. I would also have the responsibility to oversee the security of his various concerns. I think I would not only enjoy the responsibilities, but it would be enjoyable to work for the man."

"That seems like a no-brainer to me. Why wouldn't you accept such an offer?" Randi asked.

"I guess most people would jump at an opportunity like that, but I'm not sure it's what I should do. I'm living my dream now as a police officer here in Adairsville, and I'm reasonably certain, unless circumstances change, I will someday follow in my father's footsteps as chief. Then there is the other factor," he added.

"What *other* factor?" Randi probed as the waitress brought their food and proceeded to place it in front of them.

Charley waited until the waitress had left before he answered Randi's question. "If I took the job, I would have to move to the other end of the state—to Savannah."

"Why is that a problem?" Randi asked. "I would love to move to Savannah. It would be at the very top of my list for desired places to live."

"I don't know about that. I guess I'm not a city boy, and I've never really thought much about residing anywhere but right here in Adairsville. My family and friends are here, and I'm genuinely comfortable where I am – pretty much set in my ways."

"If you want my opinion, you should take it! You may never get another opportunity like that. I assure you, when the right opportunity comes along for me, I'm out of here," the young basketball coach declared.

"I know it would be the logical move for me to make, but as Davis told me, 'the logical move is not necessarily the right move.'"

"Davis is a nice guy, but that doesn't mean he's always right. He's no Solomon. You need to make your own decisions," Randi advised.

"Yeah, that's what Davis said. I need to make my own decision, but there's no reason I can't bounce these questions off a good friend."

"I'm your friend too, aren't I?" Randi asked with a smile.

"A friend, and hopefully much more," Charley responded with the most adorable smile he could muster.

Because he wanted to change the subject, Charley said, "Incidentally, I had planned to attend your basketball game Saturday afternoon since I had the day off, but that happens to be the only time I can get Davis and the others together to empty Aunt Bessie's storage unit. I guess I must miss the game to strike off the list one of my responsibilities as Aunt Bessie's executor."

"I wondered about that," Randi said. "Why did Mrs. Taylor make you executor of her estate? Didn't she have a son and daughter, as well as several grandchildren?"

"She did, but they didn't always show a lot of... let's say *interest* in her, and they haven't consistently made good decisions in life. I kept an eye out for her and gave her some time. I suppose, over the years, I gradually became her favorite nephew and she learned to trust me."

"Why shouldn't you be her favorite? You're such an adorable sort." Randi kidded him. "There have been some recent reports of attempted break-ins at that storage facility. Do you think it is safe? When I moved to town and became Barbara's roommate, I needed a place to store the junk for which I didn't have room in the apartment. I was told that was the best and safest place in town. My unit is number nine. Is that anywhere near Mrs. Taylor's unit?"

"It's just around the corner. Her space is number seventeen. To answer your question about whether it is a safe place, let me say, yes, it is. Of course, there's no place that can guarantee absolute security, but that's as secure a storage place as you will find in this town."

"It's good to hear that. The bits and pieces I have stored there are probably not very valuable, but they are important to me. I would hate to lose them," Randi stated.

"You don't have to worry about that," Charley told her. "By the way, I have the entire weekend off, and I think I'll go to church Sunday. I sort of enjoy Davis's practical lessons. Would you like to join me? We could go out to lunch after the service and even take Barbara along if you wish."

"I would like that, but we don't need to take Barbara with us. She probably won't be in town this weekend. Recently, she's left most Friday evenings and not returned until Sunday night.

Her son in Savannah seems to be pretty much tied to her apron strings, and she thinks he needs her to be there."

"I don't know all the details, but he's been through a lot recently, and she, no doubt, feels it's important she be there to help him get through it. She seems to be a super lady – a good mother." Charley added.

As the night went on, Charley's thoughts were, *she's great to look at and I do enjoy time with her, but I don't think I would want to spend my life with her.*

When Charley walked Randi to her door, he noticed Davis's Jeep was not in the drive. He wondered what his friend was up to tonight.

"Would you like to come in for a while?" Randi asked when they got to the door. "I'm sure Barbara wouldn't mind. She's probably in her bedroom with a book by now."

"A tempting offer," Charley said with a smile, "but I'd better not. You have things to do to get ready for school, and I need to get some rest before I report in tomorrow. I'll stop by to take you to church and lunch on Sunday," he told her before he put his right hand on the small of her back and pulled her a little closer to kiss her on the cheek.

CHAPTER 17

On Friday Deidre met with a student organization she sponsored. Davis considered breakfast with the guys at the Little Rock Café, but decided instead to prepare breakfast for Deidre and himself while she got ready for the day. They ate quickly to enable her to get to her responsibility on time. Davis worked at his computer on the Adairsville history book for a couple of hours before he showered, dressed and was on his way to his shop.

Janie was behind the checkout counter when he came through the door, where she gave most of her attention to her smartphone. "Good morning, Janie," Davis cheerfully greeted the young clerk.

"You sound chipper today," Janie responded. "You must have gotten a good night's sleep."

"I got a terrific night's sleep. That happens when you go to bed with a clear conscience," Davis stated while he lowered his face and raised his accusing eyes to peer at her. "What's the matter, Janie, do you have difficulty sleeping?"

"See, that's the way you are. I try to be congenial, and you pick on me, and you a preacher. Aren't preachers supposed to be compassionate and kindhearted? You ought to be ashamed of yourself." the pesky clerk declared.

"You're right, Janie. You're a good friend and I need to treat you better."

"Got you! You're so easy. I made you feel guilty, didn't I? Don't think you can go one up on ole Janie," she responded with a laugh.

Later in the morning Davis was surprised when P.W. Taylor, along with another man, entered his shop. "Hi, P.W. Good to see you," Davis greeted him. "Can I help you find anything?"

"Yeah, my friend Kenneth would like to look at your Georgia history section," P.W. spoke in a distant tone.

"That section would be right over here," Davis led them to the proper place. He tried his best to be friendly. "You guys let me know if there is something I can help you with."

"It's just a bunch of junk. There's not a book here that interests me," Kenneth said to P.W. after five minutes, and a quick survey of the Georgia section.

Davis, who took great pride in his Georgia collection heard the remark, but responded with a smile when P.W. told him, "We wouldn't spend our money on any of that junk."

"I'm sorry I don't have a thing that arouses your interest. I will work hard to improve the selection. Maybe next time you guys come in, I'll have a book or two that will appeal to you."

"I doubt very seriously that we'll ever be in here again," P.W. replied. "After we get that stuff out of the storage bin tomorrow, we plan to blow this boring excuse of a town, and you'll probably never see me again."

Davis's first impulse was, *that will suit me fine*, but he knew that was unkind and instead responded, "I'm sorry we haven't made you feel more positive about our town, P.W. It's really a fantastic place to live."

"It's maybe a good place to live if you're a hundred years old, and want to sit around and watch TV," he told Davis as he and his friend stomped toward the door. "I guess I'll see you tomorrow at about two o'clock," he muttered but did not look back at Davis.

Well, that was pleasant. I can't imagine what makes him so cantankerous. I've done nothing to hurt him and don't plan to do so, Davis said to himself. *I guess some people are just not happy unless they're crabby.*

Shortly after Davis returned from lunch he received a call from Robert Hill, chairman of the church board, "Davis, we appreciate the way you have taken the bull by the horns as our interim pastor. Michael and I would like to come by and talk with you tonight if we could." Michael Wallace was also a member of the church board. Davis's first inclination was to wonder, *what have I done now? No doubt I've offended someone.*

"Sure, we would be happy to have you. Dinner should be over by seven o'clock. Any time after that would be fine," he told the church elder.

"We'll make it seven-thirty then," Robert informed him before he ended the call.

* * *

Deidre was in the teacher's lounge between classes when she received her husband's call. "Honey, I thought I needed to give you a heads-up, I got a call from Robert Hill. He and Michael plan to come by the house around seven-thirty tonight. I'll try to get home a little early, maybe around four," he told her.

Deidre loved being Mrs. Davis Morgan every bit as much as she dreamed she would, *but it surely has increased the pace of my life*, she told herself. *There's always somewhere to go or a task to do. Not a lot of leisure time, but that's okay*, she told herself when she remembered how bored she used to get when she was single with less responsibility. *However, I did read a lot more*, she thought, with the pile of unread books she had at home on her mind. Reading had always been one of her greatest pleasures, but she was ready to sacrifice much of the time she previously had available for the life she had found with Davis. Twenty-nine years old at the time of her marriage, she had waited longer than most for matrimony. She now knew why that had been the case. She was convinced God, all along, had planned that she would be

Davis's second wife. It had always been in the mind of God. She was confident of that.

"What're you thinking about?" Deidre's thoughts were interrupted by the voice of Clare Johnson, a veteran teacher almost ready to retire. "You looked like you were a million miles away."

"I was counting my blessings. I've decided I'm just about the most blessed lady in the world," she told her teacher friend.

"Wait until you've been married for another couple of years. You may change your mind," Clare declared with a giggle.

"I don't think so," Deidre replied. "It's not just my marriage. Life is good. God has blessed me with just about all I ever wanted. I love to teach, I have super friends and a great husband. Sometimes I wonder if it could get any better."

"Maybe it can't get any better and maybe it can. I'm glad you feel as you do, and I don't want to pull you down, but you would do well to remember that sometimes life changes quickly. Perhaps it can't get any better, but it can surely go downhill rapidly. To live a life is to endure a series of ups and downs," Clare told her as she sat down in a nearby chair and took a sip of the coffee she had poured for herself.

Deidre wondered if Clare had some current crisis with which to contend. "I know that, and I hope I haven't given you the impression that my joy depends on the circumstances that come my way. I learned a long time ago that when one has Jesus in his or her life, the circumstances don't matter. Life is Christ-filled and Heaven is sure. That's what matters, not the circumstances."

"You've got it, girl," Clare agreed with a smile. "You sound like a preacher's wife or something."

*　*　*

"Do you have any idea why Robert and Michael want to see us?" Deidre asked Davis as they finished dinner.

"No, I don't have a clue. I learned through my previous ministries though, that usually, when elders want to see the preacher, it's because someone is unhappy. They don't ordinarily meet with the preacher to tell him what a great job he has done," Davis informed his wife.

"I can't imagine what they could be displeased about. Attendance has continued to be up, and the sermons have been fantastic. Everyone says so."

"I appreciate it, honey, but you are biased. You can see no wrong in the preacher, but unfortunately there're those who can see no right in him. If I've learned anything about the people who make up a church, I've learned that there are those who look for the downside and couldn't see the positive even if it's dangled in front of them. They feel they are called to straighten out all the flaws in the church and especially those of the preacher."

"But isn't that an unchristian attitude?" Deidre, ever the idealist, asked, obviously, somewhat puzzled by what Davis had just told her.

"I hope you'll always maintain high expectations for God's people, but I'm sure you understand that the church is made up of all kinds of people at different levels in their Christian maturity. Yes, such a cynical approach is unacceptable to Christ, but so are a lot of other snares in which we are often trapped. Our job as church leaders is to lead people to a more complete maturity, and from that higher perch comes change to a more acceptable attitude."

"I've got so much to learn," Deidre admitted.

"As do I," Davis responded. "We can learn together."

They shared the clean-up duties, which allowed them to get the kitchen back in order very quickly. They had just sat down when the doorbell rang. "Hello gentlemen," Davis greeted the two dignified men when he opened the door. "Won't you come in and find a seat?" Deidre offered them coffee, which they turned down.

"We are sorry to intrude on a Friday night. I know it's a time when most people sort of wind down and recover from the week. We have an elder's breakfast tomorrow and wanted to speak to you before we meet," Robert, a kindly, white-haired gentleman in his early seventies explained.

Davis had known Robert all his life, yet tonight his words seemed forced and formal, almost rehearsed. "You've not intruded. We are delighted to have you here," Davis announced, with the hope that the men would feel more at ease.

"Let me start with the assurance that we could not be more pleased with the job you have done as our interim preacher. Everyone has been buzzing about the quality and helpfulness of the messages, and of course our people have always loved you. You are our most successful Timothy, and we're proud of you. I don't know that I've heard even one complaint," Robert told them as Michael nodded in agreement.

Davis saw Deidre glance toward him with that look that says, *I told you so.* "You gentlemen are extremely gracious. If you're here to tell me you have found a permanent man for the job, I'm delighted. You don't have to let me down easy. I'm ready to step aside whenever you find the right person."

"Oh, no, that's not what this is about!" Robert excitedly responded.

"Actually, it is," Michael who had remained quiet up to this moment jumped into the conversation. "As you know, I'm the chairman of the pulpit committee, and we've found our man! The man we want for our new pastor is the man who is presently our interim minister. The committee has unanimously voted to present your name to the elders for approval, and once that formality has been taken care of, the congregation will vote."

Davis sat silently and looked at the floor before he raised his head to smile at the two men who sat in front of him. "You cannot imagine how flattered I am that you would offer me such an incredible opportunity, but you've caught me completely off guard.

There are some realities that need to be considered here. As you mentioned, I am a Timothy of this church. Some of these people changed my dippers when I was a baby in the nursery. They heard me when I cried and fussed in the services, and they're certainly aware of some of the trouble I got myself into in my teen years. Can they ever completely accept me as their pastor?"

"We considered that, and we have tried to get a feel for it over the past weeks as you have served in the interim. We are satisfied that your familiarity to the people is an asset rather than a problem," Michael told him.

The tension at that point was broken by the sound of either Barbara or Randi walking down the hallway which divided the two apartments. "The weeks in which I've functioned as pastor of this church have probably been a far more valuable experience for me than for the church. It has enabled me to rediscover that I am a pastor at heart," Davis told them. "But is this where the Lord wants me to serve? Maybe He has a preference and maybe He doesn't, but I believe I do need time to explore that question. I also need to talk with my wife; because, as you know, it's a team effort. I hope you understand that I'm not ungrateful for your support. The fact is, I'm thrilled with your confidence in me, but I think you know that I cannot give you an answer tonight. Deidre and I need to talk and, most importantly, we must talk with the Lord about it."

"We'd hoped for a decision tonight," Robert told him, "but we understand that you need more time. Perhaps you will be ready to decide in a couple of weeks," he suggested.

"Perhaps!" Davis responded. "I promise you, we'll do so as soon as possible, but we don't want to get ahead of the Lord."

They chatted for another ten minutes before Robert rose to his feet. "Well, Michael, we need to get out of here and let these newlyweds get on with their evening."

"Thank you, gentlemen. Your visit certainly has given Deidre and me an important subject to talk about tonight," Davis told them as they left the room.

CHAPTER 18

"**W**ell honey, what do you think? Do we accept this call? Are we ready for this?"

Deidre hugged her husband tightly and said, "I'm so proud of you and proud to be your wife. You know I love it here, but I don't want that to influence you. I'm ready to stay right here or go someplace else now or later. You and the Lord need to make that decision."

"*We* and the Lord will decide," he corrected her. They talked well past eleven o'clock, and left almost no aspect of the decision unexplored. They prayed and went to bed. Davis decided he now knew what Charley was going through. It was past one-thirty when Davis last looked at the clock. It had been awhile since he had found it so hard to sleep. He was sure he now knew why Charley sometimes walked around like a zombie. To make decisions that alter one's life can have that kind of effect.

Davis remembered parts of a passage of scripture from Proverbs, but he became flustered that he couldn't bring it all together in his mind. Careful not to awaken Deidre, he got up and went into the living room where he switched on a small lamp and picked up his Bible. He turned to Proverbs 2:1-6 and read, *My son, if you accept my words and store up my commands within you, turning your ear to wisdom and applying your heart to understanding, and if you call out for insight and cry aloud for understanding, and if you look for it as for silver and search for it as for hidden treasure, then you will understand the fear of the Lord and find the knowledge. For the Lord gives wisdom, and from his mouth come knowledge and understanding.*

Davis knew he needed to put his decision in the hands of the Lord and not fret over it. Finally, after he came to that conclusion and turned out the light to climb back into bed, he fell asleep.

* * *

"I can't believe that I volunteered for this duty," Charley whispered to his partner, Jed, while the two of them sat behind pieces of antique furniture in a dark storage unit. "There's not a lot of air in here and that pizza you ate earlier doesn't help that situation."

"I'm not exactly thrilled with my position so close to you either. Drink your coke and stop grumbling," Jed insisted.

"If I keep guzzling coke, I'll have to use the restroom. If you'll look around, you'll see there are no facilities here," Charley quipped.

Jed laughed, but Charley didn't see the humor of the situation. "Keep it down, will you? If anyone does come to the door, you're going to scare him away." Charley mumbled about Savannah looking better all the time.

"What are you muttering about?" Jed questioned.

"Oh, forget it," Charley told him. "I'm just thinking out loud. This was a dumb idea. No one will show up tonight."

"If it was a dumb idea, it was your dumb idea." Jed reminded him.

"Not really. It was Davis's brainchild. I just took credit for it," Charley admitted.

"Doesn't that pretty basketball coach live in Davis's apartment? I saw you at the Adairsville Inn with her recently. Is there anything serious between the two of you?" Jed asked.

"You're a really nosey dude. No, there's nothing between us. We've been out to dinner a couple of times, but there's no serious relationship in the works," Charley told him.

"You may have missed the boat with that one. She's really a looker," Jed uttered. "If I wasn't married to a special girl, I might give you a run for your money with her."

"She's beautiful all right, but I'm interested in a lot more than looks, and I'm not sure Randi has what I really want in a girl," Charley explained.

"You've changed, Charley. I remember when you made a point to date every unattached attractive girl you met. What happened?"

"I don't know. I guess I've just grown up a little. Don't misunderstand me. Beauty is still an important factor, but the person – the person inside is also important, maybe more important than outer beauty."

"Is that really Charley Nelson over there behind that dresser? It doesn't sound much like him. It seems to me that you might be ready to settle down. What about Tonya?" Jed asked. "I know you've visited with her a lot since the accident. Is she the type of girl that attracts you?"

"Quiet! I think I hear a noise outside," Charley whispered. They remained in complete silence for three or four minutes, but heard no further sound. "I guess it was nothing. Maybe we'd better cut the chatter and keep quiet," Charley suggested.

"You just don't want to answer my question about Tonya," Jed accused while he spoke in a tone barely loud enough for Charley to hear.

"It's none of your business how I feel about Tonya, but I'll tell you this, she's one of those rare girls who is more than just a beauty queen. There's more to Tonya than meets the eye," Charley told his partner.

"It sounds to me like you're smitten," Jed said with a laugh before he terminated the conversation. They sat silently for the next hour with Jed in an old chair and Charley on two stacked boxes.

Not the most comfortable seat I've ever had, Charley decided.

Charley had almost fallen asleep when he first heard the noise outside. It sounded as if someone was pounding on the door lock. He took a step to his left to nudge Jed, thinking he might have dozed off. Both officers drew their revolvers from their holsters and silently waited. The overhead door gradually moved up. With light behind him, they could see, in the doorway, a figure dressed in a black hoodie with the hood over his head.

"Adairsville Police Department... raise your hands, turn and put them on the wall," Charley shouted. The would-be burglar raised his hands and slowly turned. When he faced the wall, he quickly dropped his right hand and drew a revolver from his belt. Without turning, he pointed his gun in the direction of the two police officers and emptied the chamber. There were five shots in rapid succession.

Charley saw the felon's gun a split second before the first shot was fired, "He's got a gun!" he yelled before he got off one shot. Because he tried to duck behind a piece of furniture at the same time he fired, he either missed his target or marginally winged him. It must have been the villain's second or third shot that brought Charley down. The slug somehow found its way through the right armhole of his vest as he had his arm raised to fire. Then he was on the floor, completely oblivious to all activity around him.

Unfortunately, the fifth and last bullet fired by the nasty piece of work with the gun caught Jed in the side to penetrate the vest that was supposed to protect him. The impact caused him to spin and fall to the floor on his face. The hooded thug turned to immediately run, leaving two bleeding officers on the floor.

* * *

Jed stumbled when he tried to get to his feet. He caught hold of a piece of furniture to pull himself up. In the distance, he heard an engine start. The car made a lot of noise as it burned rubber, obviously throwing gravel as it accelerated. "Charley, where are you? How bad are you hit?" The disconcerted police officer cried out to his friend and partner as he fumbled for his flashlight. Finally, he located the light, and turned it in the direction where Charley was when all the chaos began. He saw Charley on his back on the cement floor with blood on his uniform. A puddle had already formed on the floor.

"Oh, no!" Jed cried out as he dropped to his knees beside his fallen partner. He could not determine whether Charley was still alive. He felt no pulse, but in his state of panic, he knew he probably wouldn't be able to find his own pulse. His left side was covered with blood and he was getting weaker by the second. Unable to get up from Charley's side, he fumbled for the radio he wore on his shoulder. "Officers down, two officers down at the storage facility..." is all he could get out when he finally pushed the button and spoke into the receiver. He tried to give an address and more details, but no words, only grunts came out of his mouth.

Jed lost all sense of time and was barely conscious, but he was vaguely aware of Chief Hanson in civilian clothes when he stooped beside him to push a towel tight on his wound. The chief pleaded, "Hang on Jed, the emergency people are on the way, hang on!"

Jed couldn't see Charley and he tried to ask about him, but the chief told him, "Be quiet, everything will be okay..." The last sound Jed heard before he completely lost consciousness was the sound of the siren when the emergency vehicle arrived.

CHAPTER 19

D avis was awakened by a voice and by a knock on their bedroom door which led to the big hallway that separated the two apartments. "Davis, I think someone's stealing my car!" Davis recognized Randi's voice before he sat up and then sprang out of bed. When he opened the door, Randi had a look of panic on her face. "I heard noise out front, and when I looked through the window someone was walking toward my car."

"Is your vehicle locked?" Davis immediately asked her.

"I think so. I always lock it."

The two of them walked toward the front door. Barbara had left earlier for South Georgia, but Deidre, not to be left behind, followed them. "You two stay inside," Davis instructed, when he reached to flip the switch beside the door that turned on the series of lights over the wrap-around porch. When the lights came on, Davis opened the door to go outside. Momentarily, he stood still and stared in the direction of the spot where Randi usually parked her car. It wasn't there. Randi's metallic blue Camaro was nowhere in sight, but in the spot beside her usual space was an older model Ford with a dented front fender. Davis walked out to the vehicle to look around. The overhead security light gave him a good view, but he saw no one.

"I'm afraid someone has taken on himself to trade cars with you, and it would seem you got the raw end of the deal," Davis told Randi after he returned to where the two ladies had stationed themselves. "You better call 911," he suggested to Randi who had her cell phone in her hand.

Randi, by this time, had moved to the porch steps, and stared at the old car in the driveway. Her expression hardened. "No, let's not call the police. I know who took my car, and I'll get it back," she told them. "It's a family issue," she turned to walk back toward her apartment. Obviously, she didn't want to talk any further about the matter.

"That's strange," Davis said to Deidre as they got back in bed. "I was under the impression Randi had no family in the immediate area."

"That's what I was told," Deidre responded, "but maybe we could talk about it in the morning. It's a quarter to three, and I need my beauty rest."

"I beg to differ. You have no need of beauty sleep, but it is the middle of the night and I haven't gotten much sleep up to this point," Davis said, and reached to turn off the lamp beside the bed.

It was only about ten minutes after they returned to bed that Davis's cell, on the same table as the lamp, rang. Davis had not yet gone back to sleep and wondered, *what else could happen*? He grabbed the phone, "Hello," he answered after he took an instant to compose himself. "This is Davis Morgan."

"Davis, I'm sorry to bother you at this time of the night, but this is Dean Nelson. I thought you would want to know that I just received word that Charley and another officer have been hurt. I understand they are on their way to Floyd Medical Center."

"How badly are they hurt?" Davis sat up straight in the bed.

"I don't know any of the details, only that they were injured in the line of duty. I'm on my way to Rome now. I'll let you know what I find out. In the meantime, would you pray for Charley and the other officer, who I assume is Jed?"

"I'll do that. I'll see you at the hospital," Davis said as he got out of bed to reach for his shirt.

"You don't have to do that," his friend of many years told him.

"I know I don't have to, but it's my duty as chaplain, and more than that, my duty as Charley's friend to support them in whatever way I can. I'll be there in a half hour or so," he told Dean before he hung up.

Deidre, who had followed the phone conversation as much as possible, was already out of bed and declared, "I'm going with you." In little more than five minutes they were out the front door and on their way.

While they headed west on highway 140, Davis instinctively turned left off the main road onto Rush Chapel Road which connected with old 53 near the little community of Shannon. It was a route Davis learned early in his days as a driver before the highways had been improved. He liked it in those days because there was almost no traffic and it saved him a little time. There was still almost no traffic on that route, but with the improvements of highways 140 and 53, it was doubtful that this route saved him much, if any, time. It was mostly force of habit that caused him to go that way.

They bounced a tad as the Jeep came to a high spot in the road while Davis pressed the accelerator a little heavier than he normally would on such a road. On the left, he glanced at the sprawling stone house that sat a good distance off the road. After they traveled another two or three hundred yards he saw a car that had been pulled perhaps a hundred feet into the woods on what looked like an old logging road. He wondered why a car would be parked there at this time of the night. It took a few seconds for what he saw to register, and when it did, he almost yelled to Deidre, "I think that was Randi's car we just passed."

"Are you sure?" She asked.

"No, I'm not sure, but it looked like a blue Camaro, and how many of them do you see around here?" Davis pulled his jeep into the next drive and turned around to go back in the direction from which he had just come. When he got to the place where the blue car was parked, he pulled in behind it, and got out of the Jeep.

He immediately saw the bumper sticker on the back bumper of the Camaro that read, "I play like a girl", and he knew he was right. This was Randi's car that had been stolen only a half hour earlier. Davis returned to the jeep and told Deidre, "It's Randi's vehicle all right. I'll look around to see if I can find who took it. I know Randi didn't want to report it to the authorities, but I think maybe you ought to call them. Lock the doors and don't open them for anyone but me," he instructed.

"Be careful, Davis," he heard his wife say when he reached into his own vehicle for a flashlight before he turned to go back in the direction of the stolen car.

"Don't worry, I'm not about to put myself in any danger," Davis declared.

Deidre, in compliance with Davis's instructions, locked the doors and took out her phone to call 911.

Davis pointed his flashlight in every direction, but saw no one. *He's got to be nearby. A little more than a half hour ago, that car was in our driveway. Unless someone was here to pick him up, he's still close by, and to have stolen a car only to drive here to be picked-up doesn't make any sense. He's here somewhere.* Davis continued to search. He stopped and turned off his flashlight to simply listen. After about five minutes he thought he heard someone move up ahead. He dropped down on one knee to remain quiet with his light off. From time to time he could hear a twig break or a sound that very well could be someone as they brushed against bushes, and even light footsteps.

Careful, not to make any sound, Davis who chose not to turn on his flashlight, circled toward the spot from which came the faint noises. Now that his eyes had grown accustom to the darkness, he could see from his perch on a slight rise in the terrain, the dim image of a person stooped, very slowly making his way back toward the car. Davis's eyes continued to follow the faint image, and he soon decided the man had a gun in his hand. That meant Davis had to make a move before the culprit got back to where Deidre was situated in the Jeep. He couldn't allow a scenario that could possibly put her in harm's way. He pondered how to handle the situation. Then he looked slightly ahead of him to see on the ground a three-foot piece of a limb that must have been four or five inches in diameter. Davis picked it up and found that it was well on its way to deterioration, but he had no choice. It wasn't his baseball bat, but it would have to do.

As quietly as he could Davis moved in on the figure below. He hoped the potential killer wouldn't turn his eyes to the right and spot him. Now he was within ten feet of the man with the gun and still had not been spotted. He waited there for a few seconds, only slightly breathing. He worked up the courage and then commenced. Five or six more feet and he could make his move. He would swing the stick at the man's right hand which held the gun, and hope the force would be enough to cause him to let go of the gun. He would then try to grab the man from behind to restrain him. It was a plan with which he was not completely comfortable, but what else could he do?

Just as he was ready to swing the stick, the figure in the black hoodie turned and spotted him. He pointed the gun toward Davis before he yelled. "I'll not go back! You'll not take me back!" Davis, for a second, froze. Then he nose-dived to the ground and began to roll down the slight embankment, but he knew that at this distance the car thief couldn't miss. *Lord, it's in your hands.* Davis prayed. *There's nothing I can do.* The man pulled the trigger once, then a second and third time.

CHAPTER 20

Davis was expecting to hear the gun fire, but instead heard a click and then another and another. At the same time, the man with the gun in his hand, obviously out of control, yelled, "I'll not go back! I can't go back...." Davis on his right side, on top of the ground, looked up and uttered the words, "Thank you, Lord." Apparently, there were no bullets in the chamber of the gun.

Davis lifted himself off the ground, and the young man in the black hoodie took a couple of steps toward him, again he pointed the gun in his direction. Surprisingly, he then dropped his arm, fell to his knees and sobbed, "Don't take me back. I can't go through that again...."

Davis leaned over to help him to his feet and reached for the gun, which the young man voluntarily released. Davis placed the weapon in his jacket pocket. He kept his right arm around his troubled captive; he walked him back toward where he had left Deidre. The young man kept his head lowered with his eyes glued to the ground and occasionally whimpered. He made no other sound, nor did he offer any resistance. "I'll help you," Davis told him. "We'll get you some help." As they approached Randi's car and the Jeep, Davis could see a blue light flashing, which told him Deidre had been successful in getting the Floyd county police to the scene. Because he didn't want to alarm his detainee, Davis waited until he got close to the two policemen and Deidre before he calmly called out, "I could use some help over here." All three of them hurried in his direction. With the two officers taking charge of the prisoner, Deidre wrapped her arms around

Davis and they continued to embrace for a couple of minutes. "I was so afraid for you. Why do you involve yourself in such dumb stunts?"

"I guess a dumb guy is prone to do dumb tricks," Davis answered with a weak laugh. He pulled the gun out of his jacket pocket and gave it to one of the policemen. "He gave this to me, but I don't believe it's loaded."

"Why did you steal this car?" one of the policemen asked the young man in the black hoodie

He looked at the policeman for two or three minutes before he finally answered. "I didn't steal that car. It belongs to my sister."

"Why did you bring it here?" the other policeman questioned.

"This looked like a good place to get away from people so I could think," the young man responded. "I don't do well around people."

Davis and Deidre looked at one another. Could this be Randi's twin brother of whom she was so reluctant to speak? "I believe his name is Andy," Davis told one of the policemen. "Judging by his dress, Andy may very well have been involved in the break-in and injury of an elderly lady that ultimately led to her death as well as some other break-ins."

"Could that have anything to do with the two police officers who were shot in your town a couple of hours ago?" one of the officers asked? "I think that happened in a storage compound break-in."

Davis's expression quickly changed and his whole face showed pure shock. "We don't know about a shooting tonight, but we were on our way to the hospital after we received word that a friend of ours, a police office, had been injured. We thought maybe he was in a car crash or some other kind of accident."

"I don't know if it involved your friend, but the word is that two officers in Adairsville were seriously wounded," the policeman told him. He looked at the young man Davis had brought to him and then dropped his head to look at the gun in his hand which Davis had a moment earlier given him. He said to his partner, "We had better get this guy to headquarters."

Davis, clearly shaken said, "We need to get to the hospital." He took Deidre by the hand and led her to the passenger side of the Jeep. In a few moments, they were back on the highway on their way to Floyd Medical Center.

"It's strange that it didn't occur to me that Charley could be seriously injured. I suppose, that's because he seems always to come away from such encounters with minor cuts and bruises. I guess I've been conditioned to expect that nothing serious will happen to him." Davis pressed on the accelerator. He knew he was driving faster than he should, *but this is an emergency,* he told himself. He slowed down slightly when he remembered he had Deidre in the vehicle with him. *All this could be my fault. Charley and Jed could be dead or near death at this moment, and it would be my fault. This is the last time I'll ever suggest any foolish plans to catch anyone. Who am I to think I know better than those who are trained in such matters? Father, forgive me for acting so foolishly. Please be with Charley and Jed as they perhaps struggle for their lives....*

* * *

When he got out of their vehicle at the hospital, Davis took Deidre's hand as they hurried across the lot and through the entrance that led to the emergency room. Davis looked for familiar faces when they entered the large area reserved for people with emergency patients. It didn't take him long to find the people for whom he was searching. Chief Hanson, Dean Nelson and several other people he recognized huddled in a corner. "How's Charley?" Davis asked Dean before he came to a complete standstill in front of the big auto mechanic.

"He's being prepped for surgery. It doesn't look good. They don't know if he'll make it, Davis," Dean told him and looked away when his voice broke.

Davis's heart sunk as he dropped into one of the chairs. Deidre sat down in the empty chair beside him. After he regained his composure, he asked, "How's Jed?"

"Jed was also seriously injured, but it looks like he'll pull through," Chief Hanson responded.

A few minutes later a nurse approached the group to tell them Charley had been taken to surgery. They were given directions to the proper place to wait and told they would be given periodic updates on any progress. The group of several people moved through a couple of corridors before they came to a large lounge area. Because it was pre-dawn, few people were there.

Davis was seated with Chief Hanson on one side of him and Deidre on the other. "Chief, I know you can't discuss details with me, but I have to ask, were Charley and Jed shot while they manned that storage unit stakeout?"

"Yes, Davis, that was the duty they were assigned."

"Then all this is my fault," Davis declared and dropped his head. "I'm sure you know it was my idea."

"It wasn't your fault, Davis. It was a good idea that somehow went awry. I'm the one who must take the blame if there's any to be given. I permitted it. Those two officers wouldn't have been out there in the unit if I hadn't sent them. But the person who is really at fault is the one who pulled the trigger, and I can promise you, we'll get him."

"He may already be in custody here in Floyd County," Davis told the chief. "I think a young man named Andy was the shooter. He's the brother of Randi Metcalf, the young basketball coach who lives in my apartment. He stole his sister's car, and on the way here, we spotted him. To make a long story short, he wore a black hoodie. He probably didn't know that mystery had been solved, and intended to transfer the blame for his crimes to the

Creeper. When we found him, he had a gun with an empty chamber, probably because he had used his ammunition in the clash with Charley and Jed."

"Wait a minute!" the stunned police chief stopped Davis. "Back up to the beginning and give me all the details. Tell me the whole story."

Davis spent the next fifteen minutes filling the chief in on all he could remember about the incident. He did his best to answer Chief Hanson's questions. He summed up his account with his own theory, "Andy is, undoubtedly, a young man with some serious mental problems, and possibly some type of substance dependency."

"I've got to call this in," Chief Hanson told Davis after he heard his account. "I've got what's left of my department swarming all over Adairsville searching for the shooter, and I need to contact the Floyd County people to see what they've learned from the prisoner." Chief Hanson took his cell phone from his pocket and moved to the corner of the room where he would have more privacy.

After some time, a nurse reported to Dean, "So far, so good, he's hanging in there, but it'll be a while yet before the procedure is finished."

Davis lowered his head and offered a silent prayer for both Charley and Jed. Deidre laid her hand on the back of her husband, and simply smiled at him when he looked her way. She knew that words were unnecessary.

It was more than an hour later when the doctor in scrubs came to Dean with an update. "He made it through the surgery. That's a major step, but he's far from out of the woods. Time will tell. The next twenty-four to thirty-six hours should tell the story. We'll keep him in recovery for as long as necessary, and then transfer him to intensive care," the doctor explained.

* * *

Randi wasn't surprised when she received the telephone call that informed her that her brother had stolen her car and had been arrested. "You can pick up your car if you wish, Miss Metcalf," the Floyd County police officer told her, "but for now your brother will have to remain in custody."

"I'll be there within the next hour to pick it up," She told the officer. Only minutes earlier, she'd received word from a friend, who kept close watch on such matters, the news of the trouble at the storage bins. She knew her brother was the culprit and she wondered if Charley could be one of the fallen officers. *What a loser*, she thought. *He never got anything right in his life and now he's spoiled everything for me here. I'll get my car and clear out of here. It's good that I have an ignition key for his old heap. I'll drive it to Rome, leave it there, and drive my car back here to pick up a few items before I hit the road.*

At first, Randi didn't think the old Ford would start, but finally after she thought she might have run down the battery, the engine kicked off. Though it sounded rather rough, it should, at least, get her to Rome. She looked at the fuel gage and understood why Andy took her car last night. The hand was on empty. She stopped at the Citco station and spent five dollars to put gas in the tank. *No reason to waste money. I only need enough to get me to Rome.* She wondered about the circumstances that led to Andy's arrest, and how much he had told the authorities. She needed to get her car as quickly as possible before this all blew apart.

* * *

Davis and Deidre waited with the others until they received the information that Charley had been taken from recovery to intensive care. Of course they would not be able to see him since he was on a respirator and would be kept in an induced coma for an undetermined period. It was mid-morning when they left the hospital. They hadn't thought about food in the midst of the crisis of the previous hours, but now they needed nourishment. The couple stopped for a light breakfast at a restaurant called Troy's before they left Rome.

"It's hard for me to put this together," Deidre told Davis while they waited for their food. "Why was Andy in Adairsville? Do you think Randi had something to do with the attempted burglaries and Mrs. Taylor's injury? And if so, what was the motive?"

"I don't have the answers to any of those questions." Davis told his wife. "Maybe after we get home, and I've had three or four hours of sleep, my mind will compute a little better. Right now, I can't think of anything but Charley. It'll be hard for me to forgive myself if Charley doesn't make it. It's hard enough to lose a friend, but to know that it happened because of my foolish plan, will make it even more difficult."

"You heard Chief Hanson. Nobody blames you," Deidre reminded him.

"Nobody but me," Davis responded. "Nobody blames me, but me."

While he drove to Adairsville, Davis felt tightness in his chest and had a little trouble breathing.

"Are you all right, honey?" Deidre asked as she stared at him with a look of concern on her face.

"I'm fine," Davis answered. "It's just that it's been a long and trying night."

Davis did not talk for the remainder of the trip. Deidre continued to glace in his direction. Evidently, she sensed that all was not right.

CHAPTER 21

Chief Hanson thought the young woman he saw leave the parking lot at the Floyd County jail looked familiar. It wasn't until he was inside that it dawned on him that the attractive blond who had walked rapidly through the lot was Randi Metcalf, the sister of the object of his visit. Maybe it would be beneficial to have her present when he questioned the boy, but it was too late for that. She, no doubt, was off the premises by now.

Because the crime of which the prisoner was suspected was against Hanson's officers, the sheriff readily permitted him to interrogate Andy Metcalf. The chief was informed that the detainee had not yet asked for a lawyer, and he hoped he would not do so until he had a crack at getting the whole story from him. He was taken into a small room where Metcalf was seated with his elbows on a table and his face in his hands. Chief Hanson was seated on the other side of the table.

"Son, why don't we avoid a long drawn out affair and get it over with. I suspect you are tired and so am I. What happened last night in that storage facility back in Adairsville?" The young man in the black sweatshirt remained silent while he continued to hold his face in his hands.

"You left one officer to fight for his life and another seriously injured. The best move you can make for yourself is to come clean," the chief told him.

Finally, the young man raised his head to look at Hanson and replied, "I'll not go back there. No way will I go back!"

"No way you'll go back where?" the chief asked.

"There's no way I'll go back to that prison or that hole they call an institution," he explained. "I can't do it. I wouldn't be able to stand it."

"You tell me what caused you to shoot those officers, and I promise you I'll do what I can to see that you are treated fairly," the chief told him without a lot of conviction in his voice.

"It was because I couldn't go back."

"Why were you at the storage unit in the first place? What were you after?"

"She sent me. She wanted that manuscript and refused to give me the money I needed unless I helped her get it," the young man, whose hands shook uncontrollably, bellowed. "It wasn't my fault! I couldn't go back!"

"Who do you mean when you say she? Who is she?" Hanson asked.

"She's my sister."

"Do you mean that you were sent to that storage unit to get a manuscript for your sister, Randi Metcalf?"

"Yes," the young man responded through his sobs, "Yes, my sister wanted a package from that unit. I was there because she asked me to get it. I didn't know those policemen were there."

"What was it that your sister wanted? What was in that storage unit that was so important to her?"

"It was that pile of papers she called a manuscript. If I got that for her, she was ready to give me some real money."

* * *

When they arrived home, Davis told Deidre, "I don't really have the time, but I won't be able to function for the rest of the day if I don't get some rest."

"I understand," Deidre replied. "Why don't you go lie down on the bed where you won't be disturbed?"

"No. If I do that, I'll probably end up in a sound sleep, and I need some serious time to get ready for the service tomorrow. I'll just plop down here in my recliner for a few minutes."

Deidre had some housework to do, but instead sat down on the sofa with some school work. A bit worried, she continued to watch her husband after he closed his eyes.

Not fifteen minutes had passed before Deidre heard a noise in the apartment next door. She assumed it was Randi and quietly tiptoed past Davis to investigate what she heard. She knocked on the door and heard Randi say, "Come on in, it's not locked." She was surprised to see that the young basketball coach had packed some clothes in a suitcase. Two boxes were on the sofa filled with Randi's belongings.

Deidre did not know Randi had any plans. "Looks like you plan to take a trip," she commented.

"Yeah, after all my brother has put me through, I just need to get away for a few days. With Christmas break starting Wednesday, I'll line up a sub for Monday and Tuesday, and have a nice long vacation. Maybe by the time I get back much of the trouble will have blown over, and I won't have to answer a lot of embarrassing questions."

"I understand that, Randi, but your brother may need you. I don't know how much you know about what he did, but it likely goes far beyond taking your car."

"You mean the shooting of those cops last night," she harshly responded. "When I figured out that it was him who took my car, I knew it was some kind of mess like that. This is not the first time he's been in serious trouble."

"Randi, it wasn't just two cops that were seriously wounded. It was Charley and Jed who were shot."

Randi showed neither surprise nor emotion of any kind. "I hadn't heard who the victims were, but I know I've got to get away from it all," she told Deidre while she continued to place personal items in the suitcase.

"I know it looks bad, and maybe that's been his pattern in the past, but after all, he is your brother. It would appear he has no one else to stand by him."

"You know nothing about it," she punctuated her words with obvious bitterness. "He's a mentally ill alcoholic, and I don't want anything to do with him. I plan to get out of here as quickly as I can."

Randi closed her suitcase and started to pick it up when a very pale Davis appeared at the same doorway Deidre had entered. "You need to wait for a few minutes," he told Randi, "I just received a call from Chief Hanson who told me to ask you to wait here until he arrives. He wants to talk with you."

"Well, I don't want to talk with him," Randi announced.

"It looks like you don't have a choice," Deidre responded as she pointed to the window behind where Randi stood through which two police cars could be seen. The doorbell rang and Davis immediately went to let the officers inside. Randi glanced behind her before she ran past Deidre toward the backdoor which she opened. When she started her sprint again, she ran right into the arms of two of Adairsville's finest who had stationed themselves there just seconds before.

* * *

Randi was taken to the police station where she was told by Chief Hanson that her brother had named her as the person behind his attempts at burglary. At first, she denied it, but after a lot of tough questions by the chief, she finally gave up and admitted her part. "I didn't mean for him to hurt anyone. I was horrified when I learned what he had done to Mrs. Taylor, and I had absolutely nothing to do with the shooting," she told Hanson.

"Start at the beginning and tell us the whole story," Chief Hanson suggested.

Randi began a strange story that caused Hanson to wonder how much more superficial and self-centered people in our world can become. "It started back when I worked in Bremen. There wasn't much there, so I occasionally went up the road a few miles to Carrollton for entertainment," she told him. "I went to a bar there from time to time that was frequented by P.W. Taylor. I recognized right off that he was nobody, a big mouth that would tell any lie to impress the girls. Of course, none of us paid much attention to him when he said that his grandmother knew Margaret Mitchell. I've always been fascinated with *Gone with the Wind*, but I paid little attention to him when he talked about a manuscript with the words, *The Big Four*, on the title page along with the name Peggy Mitchell at the bottom of the page. He said Margaret Mitchell had brought it to Corra Harris, a more seasoned and oft published author, for her opinion. That was pre-*Gone with the Wind*. For some reason, P.W said, it was never retrieved and ended up in the stuff his grandmother had received from the Harris estate. He claimed he had often seen it in his grandmother's attic when he was a teenager. I figured he made the whole story up."

She stopped and became silent for a few moments at which time Chief Hanson prompted, "Go on, we need to hear the whole story."

She continued, "Then when I moved to Adairsville and learned it was true that P.W.'s grandmother, as a girl, *had* known Corra Harris and Margaret Mitchell, I began to think maybe it all was true. Maybe she did have such a lost manuscript and didn't know what she had. I began to ask around and people told me, they wouldn't be surprised if it were true."

"It was about that time that Andy showed up and needed some money. I got him a motel room and bought his meals. I told him there was more where that came from if he would do what

I asked. Andy has never had any scruples, so he agreed. His job was to find that manuscript, but I never intended that he hurt anyone."

It was difficult for Hanson to believe. Mrs. Taylor was dead and two of his officers were in critical condition in the hospital because one spoiled brat yearned for a treasure that probably didn't even exist. "Tell me, Randi, what would you have done with that manuscript if you found it? Did you plan to market it, and get rich, or just keep it in your private *Gone with the Wind* collection?"

"I don't know," she answered. "I probably would've just enjoyed it for a while before I later used it to make my millions. But that doesn't much matter now, does it? I'll never have that manuscript," she said with longing in her voice.

"Not even if it exists," the chief told her, "And I doubt that it does."

CHAPTER 22

"Maybe you need to call 911," Davis told Deidre, when he returned home from the church office where he'd been preparing for tomorrow's service. He stumbled to a nearby chair into which he practically collapsed. "I don't feel so well," he said. He seemed to have difficulty with each breath. One advantage of a small town which has its own emergency service is that response time is usually rapid, and Deidre was thankful for that. Davis was placed in the ambulance, and was on his way to Floyd Medical Center in no more than twenty minutes from the time the call was made. Apparently, he had experienced a heart attack.

Deidre called to inform Amy and was in her car behind the emergency vehicle when it pulled out of the driveway headed toward Rome. It wasn't until then that her emotions caught up with her. *This can't happen. We've had so little time together. Please Lord, watch over him. I need him so much....* She prayed and wept all the way to Rome, but fought to hold back the tears as they approached the hospital. She needed to pull herself together if she was to help Davis.

The first order of business after arrival was to provide the appropriate information for the lady in the small cubical. Deidre did that in a daze. Later she hoped she provided accurate information. She was escorted to the place where she was to wait for further news of her husband's condition. It was there that Amy and Jay joined her. The two young women hugged and continued their embrace for a couple of minutes before Amy asked through her tears, "Was it a heart attack?"

"That seems to be the case, but at this point there're no certainties." Deidre responded. Thus, began the longest night of Deidre's life.

It was more than two hours later that a doctor appeared to give them a report. "Mr. Morgan is resting comfortably now, but he definitely had a heart attack which means that part of the heart muscle wasn't receiving enough blood flow. That is due to blockage which we are trying to take care of through conventional means," he told them.

"How serious is the damage?" Deidre asked.

"We don't yet know the answer to that question. I can tell you that we have taken every precaution we can, but he's far from being out of danger. When we know more, we'll let you know." Almost as quickly as he had appeared, the doctor was gone, and it wasn't until then that Deidre thought of several more questions she wanted to ask.

* * *

Davis was seldom conscious from the time he had been taken from his home. He, however, now comprehended that he was in a hospital, and he wondered where Deidre was. He tried to ask someone dressed in white who stood nearby, but no words came out of his mouth. He knew he was about to be given an injection. Maybe it was a couple of minutes or perhaps an hour later that the vivid dream began.

In his dream, he was on the track that circled the football stadium where he played his high school football, a landmark that has now been removed, but was very real in Davis's dream. To his back was a large group of people. At the front of that group were Deidre, Amy, Jay, Charley and behind them a host of people who all, in some way, had been special to him. He was surprised at how large the group was. Davis moved toward the other end of the field and left the somber crowd behind. In front of him was the most beautiful meadow he had ever seen.

Julie stood in the foreground of the meadow. She displayed that beautiful smile he could never forget. She wore the gorgeous blue semi-formal dress in which he had so loved seeing her. She remained silent as he walked toward her to the place where he could almost reach out and touch her. It was then that she held up her hand to signal him to stop. "No," she said to him in that voice he had so adored. "No, you need to go back. She needs you." At first, he thought it was Amy toward whom she pointed; but then as Jay put his arm around Amy, and pulled her close to him, he realized it was Deidre of whom she spoke. "You must go back, she needs you, as do the others," and then Julie vanished from his sight. He stood still for a moment, crushed that Julie was gone, but then he turned and saw the crowd that stood behind him and when Deidre came to meet him, the joy returned.

* * *

The doctor in the white jacket came to give Deidre another update. "We almost lost him a little while ago," he told her, "but he rallied and seems to be holding his own. We haven't given up hope. At times, we are even encouraged. It's probably a fifty-fifty situation."

That's the way it went for the next couple of days. Sometimes the doctors seemed to be encouraged and convinced that their patient would survive and at other times, there seemed to be doubt. Three times a day Deidre stood beside his bed for the half hour she was permitted to be there. She held his hand and talked to him, but there was no response.

On the third day, Dean Nelson came by with some good news. "Charley is alert and seems to be stable. It'll be a while before he is on his feet, but he is ahead of schedule."

"That's great news, I don't know if Davis hears what I tell him, but I'll share that when I see him in about forty minutes. If anything can encourage him, that will."

"We haven't told Charley about Davis yet, but I think we will tonight or tomorrow. He has already wondered why Davis hasn't been by to see him. I think he needs to know."

* * *

"To be honest with you, it's touch and go. We don't know if he'll make it," Dean told his brother.

Charley hung his head in silence and then asked Dean, "Is Deidre here in the hospital?"

"She's been here since it happened. She hasn't left even once," Dean told him.

"I would expect no less. I suspect she won't until he recovers," Charley remarked.

"There is a real possibility he won't recover, Charley. You need to get used to that idea."

"Oh, don't worry about Davis. He's a survivor. He'll be around after all of us are gone," Charley confidently responded to his brother.

"I hope you're right, but that's not the report the doctors have given us."

"Would you ask Deidre to come up here and see me for a couple of minutes. Tell her I'd come down to visit her, but by the time I got disconnected from all these tubes and wires, I doubt I would have the strength to get there."

"I'll tell her the next time I see her," Dean agreed.

"No, go tell her I want to see her now," Charley insisted.

Dean left and returned a few minutes later with Deidre at his side. "She said she could give you three minutes," Dean told him with a slight laugh.

Deidre leaned over him to give him a hug, careful not to squeeze too hard or get tangled in any of the tubes to which he was connected. "I'm so happy you're on the mend," she told him. "We were terribly worried about you."

"You didn't need to worry about me, I'm too mean to die, and just the opposite is true of your husband. He's too good to die."

"It doesn't work that way Charley. Good people and bad people die, and all those in between," she assured him.

"Maybe that's true, but if that God Davis always talks about is all he says He is, then He'll know that Davis has a lot more work to do here. He'll leave him here to do that work."

"It may seem that way to us Charley, but we don't always understand the ways of God. He may have other plans, better plans. We'll just have to wait and see," she told her husband's best friend.

They talked for a couple more minutes before Deidre kissed him on the forehead and said, "I'll see you sometime tomorrow."

After Deidre left, Charley made a silent attempt at prayer, *God, I know you're up there. I've seen You work through Davis. I know You've no real reason to honor any request I make, but this world, this community, desperately needs Davis. I need him. Please give him back to us.*

CHAPTER 23

People who wanted to check on Davis and encourage Deidre had been in and out ever since Davis was hospitalized. In addition to their kind words, they had brought Deidre food, material to read, clean clothes and some of them had prayed with her. Deidre knew the number of visitors she had seen was large, but she had no idea how many. On this afternoon, four days after the heart attack, they all seemed to show up at the same time. The room was large as hospital sitting rooms go, but today there were nowhere near enough seats to accommodate all who had gathered. Deidre looked around her to see people on the floors as well as many who stood, and, of course, the seats were filled. No doubt about it, this shy man had quietly made his mark on an entire community.

Deidre surveyed the crowd that had gathered. Of course, Amy and Jay were present as was Barbara Mason. Deidre wondered how Tonya Willis had managed to get there with casts on both an arm and a leg. There was Janie who informed her she just shut the 1902 Stock Exchange down for the remainder of the afternoon to be there. Together, on the opposite end of the room from her, stood Dean Nelson, Red Edwards, Brad Dewelt and Al Jensen; Davis's friends all the way back to high school, and now his sometimes companions for breakfast at the Little Rock. Brenda, the waitress, was in a nearby seat that Red Edwards had given up for her. Mayor Sam Ellison and Police Chief Hanson were there together and they talked; a rare occurrence. Nearby was a man she did not know who introduced himself as Bertram Shaw. He described himself as a customer of Davis's. Deidre couldn't believe that Miss Helen, now at least in her mid-nineties, had called a taxi to deliver her to pay her respects to the preacher, as she had put it. Carol from one of the businesses down the street was there, as well as two of the ladies from the Subway sandwich shop where Davis often ate lunch. The two church elders, Michael and Robert were also present.

Deidre was pleased to see George Black with his son Tommy who explained when they came in that it was Davis who had brought them back together. Tommy told her that primarily because Davis had befriended him, he was about to get his life back together. In just a couple of months he would go to Florida where he would have an opportunity for a try-out with a professional baseball organization. "Davis arranged that," he told her. Even the young policeman, Jed, who would be dismissed from the hospital tomorrow, was there in a wheelchair. Deidre knew that Charley was unable to leave his own room, but was, no doubt, there in spirit.

Deidre pondered the effect this man, Davis Morgan, had on her own life. Finally, she had found a man she could love without reservation. Here was a man she could completely trust. He had brought to her emotional security and happiness. He helped her grow in her relationship with Jesus Christ as well as a person. With him, each day was an adventure, and better than the day before. So little of their lives had been shared up to this point. *Surely there would be more! There had to be more! Lord, you can't take him. What will I have left if you take him!*

Suddenly, Deidre was ashamed of herself. *What am I saying? Regardless of what happens, I'll have Jesus, and He's always enough.* She vividly remembered her conversation with her teacher-friend Clare just a few days previously when she warned, "To live is to endure a series of ups and downs."

Deidre recalled her own words, *I learned a long time ago that when one has Jesus in his or her life, the circumstances don't matter.*

Life is Christ-filled and Heaven is sure. That's what matters, not the circumstances.

Deidre reached for the Bible that lay on the table beside her and turned it to Philippians one. She silently read the words of the Apostle Paul, *"For to me, to live is Christ and to die is gain. If I am to go on living in the body, this will mean labor for me. Yet what shall I choose? I do not know! I am torn between the two: I desire to depart and be with Christ, which is better by far; but it is more necessary for you that I remain in the body. Convinced of this, I know that I will remain, and I will continue with all of you for your progress and joy in the faith, so that through my being with you again your joy in Christ Jesus will overflow on account of me* (Philippians 1:21-26).

Deidre now realized that however it turned out, Davis would be where he needed to be. It was God who would decide if it was time to give him his reward or if his services were required for a time longer in this world. If God took him home, he would be better off than he had ever been before. If he pulled through, it was because God had plans for him. Davis would be okay either way.

For the first time since the heart attack, Deidre prayed, *Lord, he's in Your hands. You know what to do.* For the first time in four days she felt peace and contentment. Davis would either go be with Jesus which was best for him or he would walk again among them with his unique ability to affect lives positively. She knew what she would choose if it were left up to her, but if God decided to go the other way; she was all right with that too.

It was at almost that precise moment that Deidre heard one of the most beautiful soprano voices she had ever heard start to sing the words to *Amazing Grace*. She turned to her right to see that the voice was that of Brenda. Who would ever have believed that the waitress at the Little Rock had such a powerful voice? Everyone in the room turned toward her and listened as she sang, *"Amazing grace, how sweet the sound, that saved a wretch; like me! I once was lost, but now am found, was blind, but now I see."*

By the time she got to the second verse, almost everyone in the room had joined in. "'*Twas grace that taught my heart to fear, and grace my fears relieved, how precious did that grace appear, the hour I first believed.*"

Deidre could see people, some in nurse's uniforms and others who just passed down the hallway stop to stick their heads in the door as the group continued to sing. "*The Lord hath promised good to me, His word my hope secure; He will my shield and portion be as long as life endures.*" When they got to the fourth stanza, Deidre was sure the angels in Heaven had joined in, "*When we've been there ten thousand years, bright shining as the sun, we've no less days to sing God's praise than when we first begun.*"

For an instant, there was complete silence, so much so that one could have *heard a pin drop,* as they say. Then gradually quiet voices were heard here and there. Before the song there had been an uncertainty and sadness that seemed to hover over those in the room, now that sadness had been transformed, by one song, into an aura of strength and hope. People did not want to leave. It was as if they expected something special to happen – maybe even a miracle. And so, they stayed while only those with serious commitments left. After a couple of hours, everyone focused on the doctor in white jacket as he walked into the room and looked around for Deidre. When he found her, he said, "Mrs. Morgan, can I see you for a moment?" She got up to follow him out of the room to the small chapel.

* * *

Doctor Thompson instructed Deidre to sit before he pulled a chair around in front of her to seat himself. He smiled and said, "I've got some good news for you. Yesterday, I would not have given you a plug nickel for your husband's life. Today, I must tell you that the prognosis looks extremely good barring any unforeseen complications. Tomorrow we'll start to bring him out of the induced coma in which we have kept him. In all my years as a cardiologist, I don't know that I've ever seen such a quick turnaround. Now that I have told you that, I guess I must also tell you that if he turned around that quickly for the better, it's possible he could turn in the other direction, just as quickly, but I would be surprised if that happened. All I can say is that somebody must have prayed."

"You can be sure of that, doctor. There've been many of us that have prayed, and a good number of those have been prayer warriors for a long time."

"I don't doubt that for a moment, since apart from that factor, I don't have an explanation. I do need to tell you that your husband must make some major adjustments in his life. His heart is damaged, and there is nothing that can change that, but there is no reason he can't successfully deal with it. We'll tell you more about that as we get him ready for release, but that won't be for a while yet. We need to take it one step at a time."

When Deidre returned to the sitting room, all conversation ceased and every set of eyes turned toward her. Not surprisingly, it was Mayor Sam who spoke up, "Well, honey, do you have anything to report?"

"I do," she answered. "The doctor said, unless there are unforeseen complications, Davis is on his way back. He'll make it."

Immediately someone, perhaps Dean, applauded, and then there was loud applause from all over the room that lasted no less than two or three minutes. Deidre had never received so many hugs in one ten-minute span. People stood around and joyfully talked as if they were reluctant to leave. The room was electric with a spirit of thankfulness.

CHAPTER 24

The fire that blazed in front of Davis and Charley crackled and provided plenty of warmth which was needed because the thermometer on the back porch read below twenty degrees. That was well below normal for Adairsville, Georgia on Christmas Eve, and there was even some talk of possible snow before dawn. Both Davis and Charley would be limited physically for a while yet, but that was okay. Both were content after they enjoyed a perfect holiday meal with people they loved. Jay was helping Deidre and Amy take care of the dishes. Even Tonya, who had finally learned to maneuver well on her crutches, even though she would soon have no further use for them, was looking for ways to help in the kitchen.

"Will Randi and Andy face charges for Bessie's death?" Davis asked Charley who had talked with Chief Hanson about the case earlier in the day.

"After he consulted with medical people who treated her, the chief didn't think they could prove that the blow she received from Andy contributed to her death, but there'll be charges of assault related to that incident. Of course, both will be charged with the shooting of police officers. That should put the pair of them away for a while," Charley told him.

"I hope Andy gets the proper psychological attention. I almost feel sorry for him," Davis added.

"You wouldn't feel sorry for him if he had been in front of you, rapidly pulling the trigger of his gun pointed your way," Charley immediately responded.

"I guess not," Davis said with a smile. He elected not to tell Charley that he too had experienced that sensation, even though in his case the gun had been empty.

"But you're right, he's *emotionally and mentally challenged*," Charley agreed, in an attempt to be more politically correct in his observation than he had been in some other cases. "You know that he spent two years in an institution when he was in his middle teens?"

"I heard him make a statement that caused me to assume that at some point he had been institutionalized, and perhaps had also done some time behind bars."

"Yeah, but you know what...? It's different with Randi. She's just downright mean," Charley added. "You take someone with her self-centered mindset, add her beauty, and you've got an extremely dangerous person."

"You're right about that," Davis responded with a reflective look on his face. "I've seen it before. You know we had better stop talking shop before the ladies get in here or we'll be in big trouble."

"I received a call from Mr. Lipscomb yesterday," Charley told him. "He told me he would wait on me. He'll hold the job until I'm up and about again, but I told him, 'no.' Despite all I've been through recently, I love my job, and I don't think I could pull up roots to leave family and friends. He informed me it would take him a while to work through the other prospects, and that I should let him know in the meantime if I change my mind."

"Maybe you should give it more consideration. It's probably the best opportunity you'll ever have. Before all the recent problems, I hoped you would turn it down, but after what happened, I guess I can see why it might be wise to move on to a new chapter in your life."

"No, I knew all along I couldn't do it," Charley said matter-of-factly. "My life is here in Adairsville. What about you? Are you ready to take that pastor position when you're on your feet again?"

"I really would love to do that, but I refuse to fool myself. It would not be fair to the church to go ahead with it. I may never be able to go full speed again, and they need someone who can give himself fully to the work. I've told the guys to continue their search."

"That's okay. Our little town seems to be full of unsolved mysteries, and someone has got to give some attention to those," Charley laughed as he spoke.

"Not me, I'm through with that. I'm a changed man. From this point on, I'm just Davis Morgan, bookseller."

"Sure, you are. I believe that like I believe a hound dog can change his spots. You can't help it! Where there is an unsolved mystery, Davis Morgan will be somewhere in the vicinity," Charley emphatically stated with a smile that looked a little like a smirk.

"You're wrong," Davis challenged. "I'm through with that. I'll let you professionals take care of all the crime. Detective work offers no further interest for me."

"We'll see," Charley said.

"See what?" Deidre asked as the others came into the room from the kitchen.

"Oh, we were just discussing sports," Charley lied.

When they were all seated, Amy snuggled up close to Jay on the sofa and said, "Now that we are all together, we have an announcement for you." She turned toward her father and, with her mother's smile, announced, "Dad, you're going to be a grandfather."

AFTERWORD

Yes, Adairsville is a real place nestled in the foothills of North Georgia. The landmarks described in the story are actual places one may visit when captured by a longing for the small-town experience. We have heard testimony that the Davis Morgan books have brought more than one tourist to our town to find places described in the stories. Occasionally, we also hear of someone trying to identify one of the characters as a living-breathing resident of our little town. We're being truthful when we tell you that all the characters are one hundred percent fiction except when we reach back into area history to learn of some historical figure.

It's true that author, Corra Harris, lived in the Pine Log area at the peak of her career in the early twentieth century. It was often reported that she did indeed entertain the well-known people mentioned in the story, including Margaret Michell during pre-*GONE WITH THE WIND* days; however, we have never heard that Ms. Michell left a manuscript with her. But when we asked the question, what if she had? A neat story emerged.

With some strings still loose, we feel the need for one more Davis Morgan mystery. One of our fans told us recently, "I worry about Charley." Will he finally come to know the Lord? Will he find the right girl, and will it be Tonya? How will Davis and Deidre react to being grandparents, Deidre before she reaches thirty years of age? And what mystery, with its roots in the past, will suddenly emerge? Can Davis keep his vow to back away?

Maybe we can tie it up with one more visit to the little town called Adairsville.

Danny and Wanda Pelfrey
Adairsville, Georgia